Answered

S. Collin Ellsworth

Dedicated to my Lydia

1

I could only imagine what happened the day my brother Jake disappeared from the limited tales my family told me. I heard of the man in the fancy car who pulled up beside my four brothers and selected the eldest to complete "a job" for him. I wondered what my other brothers thought as they watched Jake ride away in the car. I never wanted to comprehend the helplessness my mother felt when she realized her son was kidnapped. It institutionalized her. All I was certain about the day Jake disappeared: it forever altered my life before it began. That day shaped my Christian beliefs or the lack there of.

Growing up meant losing beliefs in something we cherished. For most of us, the only dramatic revelation was that the Easter Bunny and Santa Claus didn't exist. When I was thirteen, I lost my belief in prayer.

Maybe I put too much hope in prayer. Thirteen was an unsettling time of confusion for all girls. Unfortunately, my concerns and uncertainties weren't about getting my first period and wondering if my crush liked me back. My Grandma Alice, who I lived with since I was in kindergarten, battled the final stages of cancer. My mother had been in and out of mental hospitals since I could remember. My father demonstrated his limited desire to parent again now that the living three brothers were out of the house. I did not know where I would be living by the end of my seventh-grade year.

I wasn't sure of how many Sundays I had hearing Grandma's weakening bellow, "Catherine! Get down the stairs! It's time for church!"

Despite her fragile state, Grandma Alice insisted we attend the church in Stillwater that she attended since she was young. That meant my Uncle Oswald and Aunt Rebecca had to drive up from Minneapolis to our lake house in Scandia to drive us down the icy back roads into Stillwater.

Every Sunday Uncle Oswald would grumble, "Can't we just go to the church we passed down the road?"

Grandma Alice snapped back, "It's the only church that still holds sympathy for us Rhinelanders."

Two years before I was born, the entire town of Stillwater held sympathy to the Rhinelander family. I have known this from old newspaper articles Grandma Alice saved at the end of family scrapbooks.

The Twin Cities news stations reported on location as the town folk searched for my missing brother. As months passed without Jake's returned, the city grew weary of the search and moved on with their lives. Jake disappearance was advent to the creation of the National Center for Missing Children and the AMBER alert. My family was left to continue the search with no resources. The stress tore my family apart.

Grandma Alice was to be damned if she didn't see that the first daughter born into the Rhinelander family in generations had a happy childhood. She took me in to live a life separate from my parents and three brothers. As a child, I never gave much thought about living away from my broken family. With toys, friends at school, and a safe neighborhood, I felt no need to acknowledge a different life.

When Grandma Alice got sick, I developed the awareness of all the ways she had protected me. I didn't want her to die and lose my life of content. With the limited abilities of my youth, I served as her nurse. Fueled by youthful optimism, I took on any responsibility to the best of my abilities. The realities of Grandma Alice's aggressive cancer won out. By the time seventh grade started, it was apparent that Grandma Alice would succumb to cancer. I attended school with melancholy detachment from my peers knowing that I could be removed from life at Scandia Middle School at any time.

Reluctance to actively seek friends resulted in many quiets weekends at home. Grandma Alice and I would often sit in the four season porch that overlooked Big Lake. I read my Sweet Valley High books as she sat in the adjacent chair wrapped up in blankets like a burrito. She stared quietly as the wind blew the snow off of the skeletal branches scattering the flakes across the frozen water.

One day she asked, "Do you hate him?"

"Who?" I asked.

"Your brother."

She didn't specify which one, but I knew she had to be mentioning Andrew. I didn't truly know Joseph and Nicholas. Nicholas joined the military after high school. He never came home while on leave. Joseph became an addict during high school. He dropped out and went wherever the drugs were. My rare visits with Andrew were the most contact I had with any brother. His ill-tempered girlfriend, Kirstin was always at his side. She always had a way of ruining the limited family gatherings by creating conflict with her solipsistic tantrums.

"I hate Kirstin, but I don't hate Andrew."

"I was talking about Jake."

Jake. I never dreamt that she asked about Jake. I never dare thought about Jake. I never thought I was allowed. In the rare times I came across his picture in a family album, a relative immediately shut it and told me I was lucky to be spared the pain of losing him.

"Your family was a loving family. Your mother was a very attentive mother. Your father…he wasn't always a miserable drunk. It's just that after Jake disappeared…."

Grandma's gray eyes filled with tears. I went to the kitchen and heated her mug of hot water in the microwave. I got a variety box of tea bags and went back out to the porch. I undid her blankets so her weak hands could hold the mug. She didn't take a tea bag. Instead, she continued.

"They said he was greedy. He was lured into the car by the promise of money. The boys just wanted to buy Judith an excellent present that Christmas. Every one of your brothers wanted the hundred dollars the kidnapper promised. He selected Jake. They said Jake deserved it because he was greedy to want the money. He never was! He was a loving boy."

After I had handed her a tissue, Grandma Alice wiped her eyes. She put her hand on mine.

"When Nicholas was born, Jake was upset. I asked him why. He made me promise not to tell your mom and dad. He wanted a little sister. He already had two brothers; he wanted Nick to be a girl."

This was the most that anyone spoke to me about Jake. I felt the urge to ask Grandma Alice more questions about the brother I never knew. She slumped into the soft cushions of her armchair exhausted. I pulled the lever to release the footrest. She closed her eyes and slept there most of the day.

The next day Uncle Oswald and Aunt Rebecca came to take us to church. Thus, I heard the usual banter of "Mom, I saw a nice church down the street."

"Just drive to Stillwater, Oswald! First Evangelical is the only church that still has sympathy for the Rhinelanders."
We were received by the same well-wishers: Grandma Alice's old friends, and their children. One person who didn't stop by to say hello was Pastor Kevin. Instead, Pastor Brian was going to preach. As we enter our pew, I heard Grandma's friend complaining, "He's one of those young pups that is going to tell family stories and ignore the scripture."

True to prediction, Pastor Brian starting out talking about how his wife made advent calendars for their three children. It was an engaging story, yet there was never a sermon that would maintain the awareness of my exhausted family. Uncle Oswald let out a loud snore. Aunt Rebecca nudged him awake. I felt myself falling asleep until I heard Pastor Brian's loud, exuberant voice state, "The best thing about our Lord is that he doesn't ask for presents. All he asks is that you pray! If you pray, the Lord will GIVE you gifts on his birthday! All you have to do is ask!"

I prayed as a child, but it wasn't anything beyond "Now I lay me down to sleep" and "Give us this day our daily bread". I never thought about praying for a favor. Pastor Brian preached that Christmas was a prayer free-for-all.

I bowed my head at a loss of what to pray for. There were so many things: Grandma Alice to be healed, my mother to regain her mental faculties, my brothers to come home with decent girlfriends...

Suddenly, the prayer that would be the answer to all of them burst into my mind.

"Lord. Please bring Jake home for Christmas. If you bring him home, Grandma will have renewed strength to fight her cancer. My mother will no longer be hospitalized for her grief because there will be none when he returns. My father and brothers will be able to be in the same room because they will want to be there to greet him. I will finally meet my own brother. Please, Lord! Bring Jake home!"

The winter sun shone through the stained glass directly at me as I raised my head. I knew it was the Lord confirming he heard my prayer.

Christmas came the following week. I pulled out the red and

green plaid jumper I declared childish the year before. This was a Christmas that warranted a festive dress. Jake was coming home!

Uncle Oswald and Aunt Rebecca arrived like every Sunday. Unfortunately, Grandma Alice's chemotherapy made her anemic. That morning she couldn't lift herself from her oversized chair.

"Mom, we'll just stay put today," I heard my uncle say from the sitting room as I walked downstairs. "Rebecca will put on coffee, and we can eat toast for breakfast."

"But it's Christmas!" I exclaimed. "We got to go to church!"

Everyone looked at me. Aunt Rebecca spoke, "Catherine, Grandma is weak. I don't find it necessary for her to fight the crowds of fair-weather church goers. We'll go next week."

I prayed to God in church to bring my brother to me for Christmas. If I didn't go, I wouldn't be able to receive the Lord's present to me! Jake would be waiting at the church wondering where his family was!

Grandma Alice gave a sad smile. "Oswald, I look forward to Pastor Kevin's Christmas sermon every year. Please, can I go?"

"You're not even dressed for church yet," Uncle Oswald protested.

"I'll be able to go if Catherine gets me my velour suit," Grandma Alice said.

The velour suit Grandma Alice was referring to was her magenta velour track suit. When in good health she would never dare go to church in pants. She insisted that a proper Christian lady always attended church in a skirt, hose, and heels. Her impending death made her change her priorities. I ran to her room to fetch her clothes.

Aunt Rebecca and I helped Grandma Alice get dress while Uncle Oswald started the car. Off we went into Stillwater. Grandma Alice peacefully napped next to me in the back seat. Uncle Oswald and Aunt Rebecca sat exhausted in the front seat. On occasion they would look at my excited expressions in the rear view mirror perplexed. I tried to keep my cool, but I just couldn't wait for them to see the surprise.

The church was crowded. Those who only attended on Christmas and Easter outnumbered the regular church goers. The sea of strangers flooding the lobby caused me to panic. How was I going to recognized my lost brother if the church was full of people I don't know?

Uncle Oswald didn't allow me time to observe the crowd. He quickly ushered us to the pews. We sat directly in the middle. I wanted to sit in the back so I could see everyone who entered the sanctuary. Uncle Oswald was running on the assumption that it was Grandma Alice's last Christmas and sat us down where she wanted.

Sitting in the middle had its advantages. I could turn my head in any direction without looking conspicuous. While Pastor Kevin recited his annual sermon, I scanned the sanctuary looking for a boy with reddish brown hair and a light dusting of freckles across the nose. I didn't see him. A couple of tall men to my right blocked my view of others sitting in that direction. I sat dejectedly.

Thankfully, Pastor Kevin's sermon was quick. Uncle Oswald guided us out of the pews quickly. We couldn't make the swift exit he hoped for. Friends of my grandmother and the children of her deceased ones walked over to us to wish her well. Grandma Alice graciously received their good intention. Uncle Oswald was peeved, but I was happy. With my family being the last to exit to leave the church, I could see everyone in attendance.

The crowd disperse when I saw him! The boy with reddish brown hair and a dusting of freckles across his nose was standing by the door in a red parka. I started to run to him as he was walking out the door. Then from behind me I heard, "Hey, Johnny! Wait up!"

Johnny responded with a "Hey, Tom!"

I walked back to my family dejected. Jake didn't appear. I didn't understand. I prayed. Pastor Brian told me that Jesus was supposed to give.

Pastor Kevin was still conversing with Grandma Alice. "I haven't seen Allen as of late. Not even around town. I remember he and Judith use to take the boys to First Presbyterian. Do they still go there?" Grandma Alice gave a sad smile of at the mention of my parents. "Not as much as I would like them too."

"Lost lambs eventually find their way."

Well, now, that explained everything to me. The Lord wasn't going to deliver Jake to a church he had little familiarity with. Jake must have attended the church he went to as a child. Now that church was over, there was only one place he would go to reunite with his family.

"We should go visit my parents!" I suggested when we were in the car.

Uncle Oswald breathed an exasperated sigh. Aunt Rebecca nudged him. Grandma Alice patted my hand. "It would be nice. It is Christmas after all."

It wasn't a far drive to my parents' house from the church. They only lived a few blocks up the hill from Main Street. I nearly jumped out of the car when Uncle Oswald pulled into the driveway. Without knocking I burst through the door....

"Don't you knock?!"

Jake wasn't in the living room. Instead Andrew's fat, saggy eyed girlfriend, Kirsten, was shouting at me from the kitchen. She was a hateful person who yelled at anyone at a drop of the hat. Rumor had it her family kicked her out of their celebrations because she was mean to everyone.

"Don't you have your own family?" I remarked.

"Now, Catherine," Grandma Alice said as she walked into the house. "We are all family here."

I didn't think so, but it was not my place to say. I certainly didn't want Jake to come home and see me in a screaming match with Kirsten. That was not the first impression I wished to bestow upon my brother. I left the kitchen biting my tongue as she stole my family's bread to make herself a sandwich.

I walked upstairs to at least find Andrew. Heck, for all I know, Jake might already be with him. I found Andrew alone in the room Joseph and Nicholas once shared. He was packing boxes.

"Hi," I greeted.

"Oh, hey, Catherine," he said. "What are you doing here?"

In most families, visiting each other during Christmas wasn't met with questions. Mine was an exception. My family stopped spending time together after Nicholas graduated high school. The last boy leaving met no longer having to maintain a semblance of a normal family we were prior to Jake's disappearance.

I smiled. "Just visiting for Christmas! What are you doing?"

Andrew wiped his blond colored brow on his flannel shirt. "Just clearing out this room for Mom now that she is back home."

Last I heard my mother was residing at Saint Francis Mental Hospital for hysteria.

"Is she better now?" I asked hopefully.

Andrew went back to packing boxes. "Not exactly," he said with his face turned away from me, "she is in Dad's bedroom for the time being. You could say hi to her if you want."

I walked to the master bedroom. My mother was sitting on the chaise lounge looking at the window. She wore the only outfit she possessed in the house, a white nightgown and a ratty peach terry cloth robe. Her curly reddish brown hair stood in a frizzled mess. I never saw her in any other state during my childhood.

My mother didn't notice my entrance. I walked up to her with apprehension. During her mental episodes she remained stuck in the day Jacob disappeared. She forgot she had a daughter most of the time.

She remained unaware of my presence when I was just inches away from her. I bent down to her ear. "He's coming home," I whispered. "You won't have to wait anymore."

I kissed her on the head. Her frozen face continued to look out the window. I left her believing she would collect herself when she saw Jake walk up the driveway. I needed to stall him to give her time to gather herself and become the mother he remembered. I walked down the stairs to go outside.

My father was smoking a cigarette in the garage. Uncle Oswald stood next to him shaking his head. My father shouted at my uncle with a voice bigger than his mere five foot five stature.

"Don't expect me to take care of her! That's the state's job!"

"She is your wife," Uncle Oswald said, who could maintain a voice free of ire no matter how high it's volume.

"That lifeless bag of bones is not the woman I married! She's the one who failed to look after the boys. Our son got taken! Now the state is expecting me to take care of her after they fail to keep a hospital open!"

Uncle Oswald appeared to hold out a narrow brown bag over the trash can. I could see a glass neck protruding from the top before it dropped down into the can. "I'll call the social worker tomorrow. She will know that you are unable to take care of Judith after she sees you can't take care of yourself."

"What gives you the right to come to my house acting high and mighty?"

Uncle Oswald sighed. "It's Mother's last Christmas. Can you blame her for wanting to spend the day with her sons, Allen?"

My father laughed, "Christmas! What's Christmas? You really thought you could show up and create a family Christmas? What family? You know where Joe is, Oswald? He's in jail again. I got the collect call yesterday morning! Nick, well, I don't know where Nick is. He jumped on a naval ship the minute he got the diploma. Jake is dead..."

"But he's not!" I chimed.

Uncle Oswald shook his head. My father stubbed his cigarette with a wicked laugh. "Of course, he is! You were born a girl! Now get that worthless thing out of my sight!"

Uncle Oswald ushered me back to the house. Grandma Alice, Aunt Rebecca, and Kirsten were sitting at the dinner table. Silently he motioned Aunt Rebecca to assist Grandma Alice out to the car. Aunt Rebecca complied with urgency. I stood bewildered at the doorway.

Andrew walked down the stairs. "Hey, Catherine, I found an old book of Jake's in Joe's and Nick's room. You want it?"

Andrew put the book in my hands. On the cover was a howling Jacob Marley hovering over a frighten Ebenezer Scrooge.

"Merry Christmas, Andrew" Uncle Oswald said as he pushed me out the door.

I looked back. Andrew was looking towards the garage as our father leaned over the trash can to grab his bottle. I understood that he didn't question our abrupt departure.

Grandma Alice sat in the back seat with her eyes closed. Aunt Rebecca looked ahead through the windshield. I longed to say something to break the tension yet was afraid that it would lead to another clamor.

Uncle Oswald came into the driver seat, slammed the car door and gruff, "Whatever happened to Christmas being a time for miracles?"

I spent the day in my room silently looking at the ceiling hugging Jake's book. The adults' voices filtered from the sitting room. Many of the snippets I overheard were about my father's comment that I was born a girl. My Grandma and uncle tried to keep the fact that my father was an alcoholic away from me; however, I figured it out at a young age noticing that his breath always smelt like Grandma's medicine cabinet. I wasn't stupid.

Or was I? I believed my missing brother was going to miraculously appear on Christmas. Math wasn't my best subject, but I could calculate that Jake would have been twenty-eight that Christmas. If he were alive, he would have the means to return home a long time ago.

It wasn't unusual for girls my age to put their fate in the impossible. Girls a half a decade older than me asked a magic eight ball if their crushes liked them or played with an OuiJi board in hopes to speak to Marilyn Monroe. In a rational mind, I would never have taken stock in Pastor Brian's sermon. I couldn't deal that Grandma Alice was dying. Pastor Brian gave me false hope. That was all I had, hope in a hopeless situation. Having a false hope made me the happiest I had been since Grandma Alice's diagnosis. Like coming down from a chemical high, I became more depressed than I was the day I said that prayer.

Grandma Alice's weak voice called for me from her bedroom. I entered to find her propped up in a buddle of blankets. She still wore the pink velour track suit.

"Oswald and Rebecca left," she said when she saw me in the doorway. "Rebecca wanted to check in on you, but you know Oswald. He thinks it's best just to leave things be."

I shrugged. I knew my family better than the adults thought. Grandma Alice motioned me to the bed. As the child I was, I wrapped myself in her frail embrace. She peered at the book I was still holding.

"What is that?"

"'A Christmas Carol.' Andrew gave it to me," I mumbled, "he said it used to be Jake's."

Grandma Alice's hand slowly stroked my hair. "People say that Jacob Marley is a scary character. I never thought so. Jacob Marley cared for Scrooge so much that he came back from the dead to save his friend from falling into the same horrid fate he did. In reality, friends do the opposite. Misery loves company."

I grunted in response.

"I heard what your father said," Grandma Alice whispered. "He didn't mean it."

"Was I supposed to be a boy?" I asked.

Grandma Alice sighed, "It was just a very complicated time when your mother was pregnant with you."

I understood, "Hope can make people believe crazy things."

Grandma Alice chuckled, "I suppose so."

She patted my head like she did when I was little and needed help falling asleep. I felt safe to ask the question I avoided the prior three months, "What's going to happen to me when you go?"

"Don't you worry," Grandma Alice said, "You will be well taken care of."

Grandma Alice died the following February. After her death, I discovered that she had investment accounts for all of her grandchildren to fund their college education. None of my brothers went to college. All five of the Rhinelander accounts were signed over to me to attend boarding school in England. Aunt Rebecca stayed with me in Scandia until I completed seventh grade. She helped me prepared for my move.

The day I left for England was the day I left my family without looking back. My family distanced me from Jake's tragedy when I lived a few towns away. I saw no reason to maintain a relationship with them while living on another continent.

I didn't think of the Rhinelanders in the two decades I lived in England. I finished school, went to college, met a man and had children. When my husband's job transferred the family to North Dakota, I didn't expect Jake to appear in our life.

2

No matter how tiny they made telecommunication devices, nothing could compensate for a teenager's lack of discretion. Every class I made a habit of walking the room as I taught my students to ensure that their attention was on the finer points of seventh grade English. During my first year, I confiscated fifteen smartphones a day. This particular year, I averaged daily with only two. Even without smartphones out, my students were distracted. It was the last class before Winter Break.

Trent Lockman's phone let out a chirp. I held out my hand. He placed it in my open palm. As a teacher, it was my duties to ensure the content of the text was appropriate.

"Spanky farted?" I read before putting the phone in my pocket. "Well good for him."

"Her," Mia Vellon dryly corrected. "Spencer Anderson is an eighth-grade loser who refers to herself in the third person as 'Spankey.' I can't believe that Trent is friends with her."

"She is friends with my sister!" Trent exclaimed, "I can't ignore her! She tattles to my mom when I do."

Mia started to open her mouth. I put my finger to my lips.

"Okay, everyone, we will forget about Spankey," I announced, "Her flatulence will not be on any exam. Now, where were we?"

I looked down at my worn copy of "A Christmas Carol" and continued the lecture. "What makes 'A Christmas Carol' culturally significant is that it changed the meaning of Christmas to what we know of it today."

"Charles Dickens created commercialism?" Leif Wilson joked.

"Hilarious, Leif," I chuckled. "However, I heard about your churches' youth group's visits to the Sheyenne Care Center last weekend. I don't believe that you think Christmas is about materialism."

"That was no big deal," Leif replied, "We just sang hymns for old people."

"You gave your time," I pointed out, "which is arguably the best gift ever. Class, Leif may have mentioned how modern media turns the meaning of Christmas. You all undoubtfully been lectured that the real meaning of Christmas is giving. Before Charles Dickens' writing "A Christmas Carol", Christmas a simply a day of reflection and prayer…"

"As it should be" Holly Shuler piped up.

The class groaned. Ninety-nine percent of Valley City's citizens believed in Christianity. One hundred percent of the same population thought Holly took religion too far.

"Okay, Holly, out with it."

Holly pushed her long blond hair over her shoulder. "In England, you may rely on novels to remind yourselves the true meaning of Christmas. Here in North Dakota, we turn to Jesus, the real meaning of the season."

A year back in the Midwestern United States didn't fade my accent, but it did fade my English manners. There were times I just wanted to whack that girl on the head with a ruler, which I never seem to have on hand. I kept reminding myself I was the adult in the room and let Holly's comments go in one ear and out the other.

"Thank you for your comment, Holly. Like everything in the culture of human existence, Christmas evolved…"

"Excuse me, Mrs. Mulroney; I am not going to allow my fellow students be preached about Christmas by someone who doesn't attend church."

The hazard of living in a small town is that people know your business. By simple deduction, my students figured out I didn't attend one of Valley City's twenty churches because I never came up in the conversations about their Sunday mornings on Monday. Since it is forbidden to discuss religion in North American schools, my lack of spirituality never was an issue. Even on that day, I knew I didn't own my students an explanation. I still don't know what inside me broke from reason.

"Okay, Holly, you believe that Christmas is about prayer and God answering them?"

"I do."

"Well, I have a story that will tell you otherwise."

I rolled up my sleeves as I walked to the front of the room. Leaning on the front of my desk for support, I told my story.

"When I was in seventh grade, I too believed that God answered prayers. That Christmas, I prayed for God to bring my brother Jake back home. I never knew Jake. Somebody had kidnaped him before I was born. In fact, tomorrow will be the anniversary of that tragic day. The police never found his body; therefore, I thought he would be able to walk into my church that Christmas. He didn't, nor did he any of the following Christmases. Thankfully, my alcoholic father told me he was dead. It freed me from the burden of needlessly waiting for a brother who will never come."

"What happened to him?" Amy Tinkenbaum whispered.

"I don't know," I answered, "all I know is that if he were going to walk through my front door, he would have done so. He's dead."

The silence in the room was deafening. Each one of my students stared at me with motionless faces. The air felt thick. Suddenly, the beeping from a delivery truck outside broke the oppressive quiet. Mia put her head down. Amy started to cry. The boys took out whatever electronics they had, except for Trent. The clock ticked. There were fifteen minutes left to class. I couldn't face my students for fifteen seconds.

"Class dismissed."

Wordlessly, my students gathered their things and headed for the door. Trent gave me a sheepish look as he passed me. I handed him his phone. The students filed out. The door quietly swung shut. Then I heard the buzzing of their whispers outside. I knew the gist of what they were talking about, "what the hell just happened"!

I sat at my desk with my head in my hands. For twenty years I had managed to keep Jake in the back of my mind. For the life of me, I couldn't understand what it was about Holly Schuler's routine attempt to preach caused me to snap that day.

My phone vibrated in my purse. My husband, Tim, texted me that he had taken our son home for school. As I read the text message, the bell rang to dismiss the students from the school grounds. I breathe a thankful sigh. Normally, I would have to run out at the first ring of the bell to pick up my son in time; but, I couldn't face my students again today. At the first moment of quiet, I grabbed my coat. It was fifteen degrees outside. I doubt my students had lingered outside on the grounds. Those who lived near Central Ave and Main Street quickly walked home on the chilly days.

I went down the halls and out of the front door. A blue knitted bubble head was waiting at the bottom cement step. "Hi, Mrs. Mulroney. Are you walking straight home?"

I hesitantly answered, "I am, Holly."

"I'll walk with you."

Damn, why did it happen to be the student I wanted to avoid waiting for me? Unfortunately, Holly wasn't just my student. She was my next-door neighborhood. Typically, she went to hang out with Amy Tikenbaum after school. Holly apparently had some motivation to blow off her friend and wait for me in the cold. As her neighbor, I had no choice but to walk with her if I wanted to see my family in the next ten minutes. As her teacher, I had to maintain a friendly demeanor the entire time. With our first step, Holly began her conversation with her characteristic purposeful manner.

"I just wanted to tell you how sorry I am about today. Nobody around here knew about your brother. Valley City doesn't get much news about England."

Because I still spoke with an accent, my students assumed I was English. Since my boarding school became the home Stillwater, Minnesota wasn't, I never felt the need to correct anyone's assumptions. If anything, I played up my British persona to validate them.

"That's quite alright, Holly. I behaved rather inappropriately. A teacher never ought to entertain her students with emotional outbursts. I need to be the one apologizing for making the class uncomfortable."

"It's not that we were uncomfortable," Holly replied, "we were all sad. It must be horrible not knowing what happened to him."

"I never knew Jake, Holly; therefore, I truly never have a reason to think about it."

"You have to care enough that you prayed for his returned."

"I was a child."

"Clearly it matters to you now..." Holly said in a quiet yet scolding tone.

We approached the footbridge that look towards Valley City State University. I wanted to be done with the conversation by the time we turned onto Thirty-Third Street and head for our homes. I stopped and leaned against the rail. Holly followed suit.

"Holly, I appreciate that you took the time to wait in the cold and give me your apology. I apologize for behaving as badly as I did. Adults' burdens should never trouble children. However, let my outburst in class be a lesson for you. Whereas it is good that you have strong convictions, you can easily cause problems when you press them upon others. A person's concept of religion is developed from their life experiences. You don't always know the life a person has led. In the future, I suggest you save your arguments for whenever you meet your friends at Dutton's café rather than disrupt class."

Holly looked down at the frozen Sheyenne River. "Understood." As soon as we continued to the cross the bridge, she immediately said, "Well, we aren't in class now. I need to tell you that God does have a purpose for everything. We may not understand it, but we always have to trust in it."

How I wished I could believe Holly. I smiled at her. "Come now; you don't need to spend your youth comforting people in things no one can control."

"I won't have my youth as of tomorrow," Holly proclaimed. "I'm turning thirteen!"

I remembered reading on her transcript that Holly's full name was Holly Noelle Schuler. I should have guessed she was born near the holidays. "Congratulations. That is a very grown up age."

"It's going to be weird celebrating tomorrow knowing that you are next door feeling sad," Holly murmured.

At first, I didn't know whether to chuckle or roll my eyes. I looked at her face and immediately felt bad when I saw her sincerity. Holly thought it was her Christian duty to take on the suffering of others.

"Don't worry about me," I said as we turned down our street. "I don't think about that day. I will be with my family tomorrow. We are probably driving into Fargo to pick up something for my hoity-toity sister-in-law from a snooty department store that won't be to her liking."

"Well, if you decide not to drive to Fargo, I'll be having a party at Pizza Corner. Bring your family!" She called out as she ran to her driveway.

"Happy Birthday," I called out as I approached my driveway. I put my key in the lock and took a deep breath. The school day was over, and I intended to put it past me.

3

My seventeen-month-old daughter, Maggie, came running to the door clad in only her diaper.

"Marguerite Alice!" I laughed as I embraced her, "Don't you think we ought to put you in some clothes?"

"No!" Maggie giggled.

Maggie ran into our living room. Moving five feet away from the door, I realized why Maggie undressed. The house was an oven. Within two seconds, I sweated through my coat. Promptly taking it off, I followed Maggie into the living room. Tim was sitting at the artist desk looking at his notebook computer laughing.

"If you are laughing at our ridiculously high electric bill, I don't share your humor."

Tim continued to laugh. "My old mate, Mac, just blew an air biscuit in some bloke's face at the pub. Now he is getting his arse kicked! There's a live feed on Facebook."

I rolled my eyes. "Which dirtbag is it? MacDonald or MacDougal?"

"MacDougal," Tim answered.

I bent down to kiss Tim on the head. I saw he wore a thin fleece pullover under his wool sweater. From the computer screen, I saw MacDougal got punched in the face.

"The sad thing is that old Mac doesn't realize that his actual issue isn't that he's always being punched but that he's in his thirties and farts in people's faces at pubs."

Tim shrugged, "We all have issues."

"True," I said picking up the unopened box of insulating plastic for the windows. "Yours is being unable to afford the electric bill because you insist on cooking a pizza in the living room. When are you going to cover the windows?"

"Jacob said that he was going to help me," Tim explained.

Grabbing Maggie, I walked upstairs shaking my head at the idea that my husband needed our six-year-old son to insulate our house. Jacob was in his room talking. I peeked in to find him alone holding his book. Jacob's school counselor said that imaginary friends were common at his age. Considering how he moved across the Atlantic, it was expected that he processed his feelings such as children do.

I took Maggie to her room to dress her in a sleeper. Jacob's voice floated through the thin walls.

"If Mum wanted to name me after a book character, she should have named me Harry Potter instead of Jacob Marley. Then Aunt Anna would give me seven different books by now instead of the same old book for every birthday."

I chuckled at the mentioned of Tim's sister. She married into the House of Lords in England. Instead of being the beloved wealthy aunt who gave cool presents, she was the vial relative who thought we should be humble enough to be thankful for a piece of dryer lint from her. Every year she gave Jacob a copy of "A Christmas Carol".

"I don't know why she named me Jacob Marley Mulroney....I asked why and she said she really likes the stupid book....Dad insisted that my name was supposed to be Timlin Ryan Mulroney Junior....Timlin is not a dumb name; it's my father's name....Well, Jake is a stupid name..."

I zipped Maggie's sleeper and carried her with me to Jacob's room. Jacob was on his bed holding a book while wearing mittens. A blast of chilly air hit me hard as I entered. I had to step back immediately from the doorway. Jacob's room was notoriously cold. The house we rented was built in the early twentieth century. I expected the heat from our electrical unit to not distribute efficiently; yet, the temperature contrast between Jacob's room and the rest of the house was drastic. At times, you needed to wear a winter coat to stand in there comfortably.

"Hey, Mum," Jacob called out.

"Hi, Darling," I answered, "your father needs your help covering the windows. Can you come downstairs? We also need to decide what we are having for dinner."

Jacob walks out of the room. I follow him out and down the stairs.

"Can we order Hawaiian pizza?" he asked as we entered the living room, "I like that kind."

"We are not ordering from Pizza Corner," Tim called out.

"But it's Friday," Jacob protested, "We order pizza on Fridays."

"Yes," I agreed.

Tim pulled out the insulating film from the box. "I'm sick of pizza."

"I wished you would have told me that you didn't want pizza," I said, "I would have stopped at the taco shop on the way home."

"I'm sick of tacos too," Tim complained, "all you have wanted to eat since we moved to the States are pizza and tacos."

"Those were two things you couldn't eat on the cheap in Europe," I said.

"We could in Italy, but you didn't like their pizza," Tim replied.

"Well the Italians didn't know they were supposed to process the tomatoes into a savory sauce."

Jacob and Tim stretch plastic over the box window in the kitchen. As Tim placed adhesive on the frame, he asked, "What do you want to eat, Jacob?"

"How about fish and chips?"

"Where do you think we are?" Tim replied.

"In a house with fish sticks and French fries in the freezer," Jacob answered matter-of-factly.

"Fish and chips it is," I said turning to the fridge.

"That is not fish and chips," Tim muttered behind my back. "It's breaded overly processed sea meat."

With Maggie playing securely in her highchair, I heated up dinner in the oven. Jacob and Tim managed to cover the one window before Tim became frustrated with the flimsy plastic.

My boys soon were sitting at the table playing with the baby. I stared at my family lovingly. If one looked at my Black Irish husband and children with their wavy black hair, pale skin, and blue eyes, no one could tell they were mine. Despite looking differently from them with my reddish-brown hair and root beer colored eyes, I couldn't imagine fitting in with any other family. With them, I was home.

Tim came to bed after rocking Maggie. I sat up reading Jacob's newest copy of "A Christmas Carol." Tim crawled into bed wearing long underwear underneath his flannel pajama set. He reminded me of a mountaineering Carey Grant. Despite growing up in the constant damp chill of Ireland and England, the sharp cold of a North Dakota winter shocked him. He insisted on sleeping underneath two blankets, a quilt and a down filled comforter. I slept in an old t-shirt and yoga pants in an attempt not to sweat while sleeping next to Tim.

"Why are you reading Jacob's book?" he asked.

"Because he had no interest in it," I answered, "He hated that it had more words than pictures. We read 'Captain Underpants' instead."

"He's sick of that book," Tim said, "You've read it to him from the minute he was born."

Jacob was born on Christmas Eve. The moment the midwife put Jacob in my arms, I immediately uttered, "Welcome to the world, Jacob Marley Rhinelander."

"Uh, Ketty," Tim said, "I was going to give him my name."

"Welcome to the world, Jacob Marley Mulroney."

"Catherine, that is not my name."

"Shut up, Timlin, I just gave birth...."

Tim had been my best friend since I moved to England. I hated him when we first met. He was a drunken spoiled son of an Irish banker. I merely tolerated him because he was the stepson of my mentor, Marguerite Mulroney, who taught literature at our school. Marguerite was the blond petite English rose who took me under her wing. Since my family became nonexistent after Grandma Alice's death, Marguerite became my surrogate mother. I stayed with her during school break. She took Tim in during holidays despite separating from his father. Eventually, I came to learn that Tim and I had a similar family background. His family shunned Tim for being born a boy three days after his sister Emily died from leukemia. He was supposed to be born the sister with the life-saving bone marrow. Despite his British arrogance paired with his Irish temper, we bonded because only the other understood want it was like to be born the wrong gender after a beloved child died. We stayed friends after he returned to Ireland for college and I went on to attend a university in Middlesex.

Saint Patrick's Day before our college graduations, Tim called me and announced a drunk driver stuck Marguerite. She died later that week. Tim's father gave her a traditional Irish wake. I joined Tim in drinking away our sorrows. The next day I awoke naked in bed next to him. I snuck out before he awoke with the intention of pretending that the event never happened. Three weeks later, I missed my period.

We agreed to continue through the pregnancy and raise the baby together. I gave birth on Christmas Eve. Tim and I loved our son immediately, yet we were not in love with each other. I imagine an even tempered responsible man for my husband; however, English men were very much obsessed with the concept of pedigree and unwilling to take a woman with a bastard to be his wife. Tim eventually grew up by hitting the books instead of the bars. We enrolled in the MFA program at the University of London. With our studies and parenting Jacob, neither of us had time to date. Our proximity resulted in my pregnancy with Maggie. Afterward, Tim found a job as the assistant community arts director at Valley City State University, which he got because he claimed he'd be moving a family into Valley City. We married to grant him a VISA and moved to North Dakota six months before I gave birth to Maggie.

Now we lived in a rented fully furnished house where the owner thought peach walls and blue and green plaid curtains made for a visually pleasing palette. The winter winds penetrated our walls. I often woke up twice a night due to the house settling. This house was my first true home, with Tim's banal criticism of what I read and all.

"Sure, everyone likes 'A Christmas Carol.' It's a classic. I just don't get why you regard it as a religious book."

"A religious book?"

"Seriously, Catherine, you act like Jacob Marley appearing before Ebenezer Scrooge was the second coming. I never understood why the character held such meaning to you."

I held the book to my chin. I never could articulate my feelings for Jacob Marley. If I could, no one would understand; therefore, I didn't bother to try. Instead, I reached up and turned off the wall mounted lamp on my side of the bed.

Tim turned off his light with a click. I turned to the side away from my husband then shut my eyes.

"Ketty?"

I groaned. Tim gave me my pet name back in school in a drunken attempt to call me Katie, which I hated. Now, he used it when he sincerely wanted my attention during times I wished to be left alone.

"What?" I groaned.

"I was talking to Jacob's teacher today. She said that there wasn't a Jake or another Jacob in the entire first grade."

"So?"

"Well, Jacob has been talking about doing things with a kid name Jake. I would like to know who my kid is playing with around town. I have yet to meet the kid, have you?"

"I heard Jacob talking to him while changing Maggie."

"There wasn't anyone in the house but us?"

I rolled my eyes. Having an imaginary friend was a rite of passage during childhood. I never understood why most parents tended to freak out when their children created one believing that it demonstrated a child's lack of social skills and possible delusional tendencies.

"Jacob is just processing his feelings about adapting to a new culture."

"You think that Jake is imaginary? Well, what about Jacob talking about playing hockey and joining the Boy Scouts? Who did he get those ideas from?"

"From living in the Upper Midwest," I answered. "Seriously, Tim, you got to lighten up. I understand that you want our son to play soccer..."

"Futbol."

"The game where the players kick the black and white ball!" I exclaimed, "I think this 'Jake' is Jacob's projection of his American self. He senses you don't want him to become Americanized; yet, he wants to fit in with his peers. I bet if you start accepting his new North Dakotan lifestyle, 'Jake' will disappear...."

With that statement, the memory of today's classroom rant came into my mind.

"You alright, Ketty?" Tim asked, "You got quiet all of a sudden."

I could have pretended to be asleep, yet Tim would have poked me until I answered the question. He never liked his curiosity go unsatisfied, even about matters that were none of his concern.

"Nothing!" I whispered irately. "I had a bad time during my last class; that's all."

"What happened?"

"Nothing really, just the Schuler girl was attempting to preach about how Christmas is about Jesus and not about 'A Christmas Carol'..."

Tim snorted, "She sure told you."

"Not exactly, I ended up ranting to the class about how prayer doesn't work using my brother's disappearance as an example."

"What?!"

"Shush," I whispered, "You'll wake up the kids!"

"Seriously, Catherine, you most likely have gotten us run out of town. Should I expect a mob with torches and pitchforks when I get the mail tomorrow?"

"Don't be ridiculous," I said.

"You are the one warning me not to attempt to change the North Dakotan culture with my European intellect."

Tim's point was valid. He struggled with the notion that he wasn't going to form his version of the Bloomsbury Group in Valley City. Whereas the citizens of Valley City did think, the people were more so doers rather than thinkers. The people here only discussed a point until an action was decided, even if the only action was to pray. Not once had a person been run out of town. Midwesterners passive aggressively shun noncompliant citizens. I didn't mind given I hated being social.

I turned away from Tim to sleep. As I drifted off, my students were actively posting prayers for me online on their social network pages. I certainly would never have guessed what the ghastly miracle

that was to come.

4

On Saturday, Tim and I took the kids to the West Acres Mall in Fargo to buy gifts for Tim's snooty family. Tim's living siblings, Anna and Mark, commented how the decorative glass bowls I purchased from Valley City's antique stores last Christmas were not well received. Anna went as far as to mention that if we couldn't afford new things, I shouldn't be giving away what were "obviously Catherine's tacky family heirlooms" and forego gift giving. I'd take Anna up on her offer however, Mark whose hobby was trading foreign currency, would always send us the foreign money with the highest exchange for the American dollar. If we bought gifts for one sibling, we had to buy for the other. Therefore, it was off to the department store to overpay for a designer label that would fit Anna's taste.

Our trip to Fargo was the North Dakota equivalent to my childhood trips to Minneapolis with Grandma Alice. The children enjoyed going to different stores, playing at the indoor playground, and eating burgers and milkshakes at Kroll's Diner.

Later that evening, Tim went to get the mail while I put the kids down for bed. As I read Maggie a story I heard, "Oh, Ketty, the Valley City moral decency police left some mail for you."

The "Valley City Moral Decency Police" was what Tim dubbed the anonymous group of neighbors who stuffed our mailbox with swimming trunks after our family's first trip to the community pool. I was afraid people would be staring at my overdue pregnant stomach. Instead, Tim's European issued Speedo caught the town's people's attention. In the Upper Midwest, people anonymously dropped off solutions to their issues on people's doorsteps to avoid conflict.

I looked down at the table. Tim laid various pamphlets about the benefits of prayer. I chuckled, "It's just the town showing they care. As a teacher, I'm touched. I didn't know my students were listening to a thing I've said."

"If you say so," Tim shrugged as he retired upstairs.

The next afternoon I set out to do laundry after putting Maggie down for a nap. Tim prepped the gifts for his family to take to the post office the next morning. Jacob practiced shooting hockey pucks against the garage. Thankfully, our garage door needed a new coat of paint. Any chip caused by the puck hitting the door would be covered in the spring.

I sat down in front of our television to fold clothes while watching a trashy reality show I'd never admit I like. From the corner of my eye, I saw the red snow shovel moving across our lawn. I got up to look out the window as Jacob smacked the shovel against his twig fort, scattering the branches across our yard. I immediately ran to the back door.

"Jacob Marley Mulroney! Come over here!"

"I can't, Mum! I need you to come over here and help me!"

"Help you with what?"

"Digging a hole!"

Had my son lost his mind? I went to the closet and grabbed my boots and blue parka. I pulled my red hat and mittens from the parka's pockets. My pensive son waited as I trudge through the snow.

"Jacob?" I asked, "What are you doing with the snow shovel in the back yard?"

"Jake told me told me your Christmas present is buried here."

"Jacob! Jake is not...."

Cognitively I had no problem reminding my son that 'Jake' was imaginary. My body let words died in my throat. Unaware of the sudden disconnect from my rational mind, I blurted, "Get me an actual shovel!"

As Jacob ran to the garage, I continued to remove the twigs with the snow shovel. Jacob returned from the garage with the steel rounded point shovel. In fear of him being pelted with flying dirt, I shooed him inside.

The twig fort Tim and Jacob made during the fall insulated the earth beneath. I broke ground quickly. The earth was heavy. My sides cramped in no time as I lifted piles of earth. My rational mind attempted to connect to my body to inform me that digging up my backyard was a fruitless endeavor lacking all reason. A force beyond my own will moved my arms to dig.

"Jesus Christ, Catherine!"

I looked back to find Tim standing behind me with his wool jacket and loafers. Embarrassed, I looked away to the small hill of unearthed dirt I created.

"'Jake' said that there was a present for me," I explained.

"Therefore, you are ruining our yard?!"

There wasn't a sensible explanation; therefore, I continued to dig in hopes of uncovering one. Tim watched me dumbfounded as I continued to dump dirt, turning the hill of dirt into a mountain.

Suddenly the shovel vibrated with a ping. Tim bent over my hole. He dusted dirt away revealing a familiar gold-plated insignia.

"That's a Boy Scout belt buckle!" I blurted, "Each of my brothers had one."

Tim ran his hand to the side of the buckle. He got up reaching for the shovel. Walking to the other side of the hole, he pierced the earth diagonally near the buckle. He lifted the patch of dirt gently. Brushing off the loose dirt, Tim revealed a brown piece of leather. Tim tugged on the belt buckle. When the belt resisted his pull, Tim dug the dirt with his bare hands. Peering down, we saw what appeared to be a broken pelvis bone. Tim wiped the fog from his glasses before confirming the gruesome sight in front of us. "Catherine, I think we need to call the police."

We went inside the house where Jacob was occupied watching cartoons. The sounds of Maggie's cry vibrated the monitor. We both looked at Jacob. Neither of us wanted him to be privy to horrors underneath our backyard.

"Hey, Jacob," Tim called as he took off his coat, "I need you to help me change Maggie."

"No thank you," Jacob answered, "That's Maggie's stinky cry. I don't want to touch poopy diapers."

"You are not going to touch poo."

Jacob reluctantly followed Tim upstairs. I walked to the refrigerator where the Valley City Service numbers were posted. I dialed the nonemergency number for the police department. Whoever was buried in our backyard was beyond the help 9-1-1 provided.

"Valley City Police Department. Stiejim speaking."

I groaned. I have worked with Chief Bruce Stiejim in the past on the community anti-drug action programs through the school. He always lit into me if I made a small cultural gaff during meetings. I thought he'd be spending his Sunday ice fishing instead of answering the station's phone. This Sunday wasn't my lucky day.

"Hello Chief Stiejim, this Catherine Mulroney. My husband and I have made a ghastly discovery in our backyard."

"Whatever could it be, Mrs. Mulroney," Stiejim mocked.

I sighed. Knowing that I haven't assimilated back into Midwestern customs at Stiejim's desired rate subconsciously brought out my English style of speech. Stiejim was supposed to be a civil servant who was to help anyone in need, regardless of their accent.

"There appears to be a skeleton in our backyard."

"A skeleton in your backyard?"

"All we have found is part of a pelvis bone," I answered, "but there could be more. We just haven't dug enough, I guess."

"You were digging in your backyard in the winter?"

"Quite right."

I heard the phone being set down then a loud knock on the door. "Hey, Paul, are you in? I need you to come with me to the Han house...you know why."

Stiejim returned to the phone. "Alright, Ms. Mulroney, we will be at the house in ten minutes."

Bruce Stiejim pulled up to the driveway in his unmarked police car wearing plain clothes. Behind him, Paul Nygren drove in the Barnes County Sherriff car wearing his uniform. The separate law enforcement entities shared the same building. From the window, I saw Sherriff Nygren start to approach the front door. Stiejim proceeded to the backyard. Nygren followed without notifying me they were there.

I went to the living room window that faced the backyard. Stiejim and Nygren walk to the hole and bend down. Hearing footsteps from behind, I turned to face Tim as he walked towards the window.

"The kids are hanging out in our room. Maggie is watching cartoons on my tablet, and Jacob is playing video games on my phone. Are the police here?"

"See for yourself."

Tim peered at Stiejim and Nygren crouching over the hole. "Are you going outside? You never leave cops on your property unattended, Ketty."

I groaned as I opened the back door. The North Dakota wind whipped my face hard. Stiejim and Nygren appeared not to notice the huge gust that whipped a layer of snow into the air. They were deep in their conversation unaware that I was approaching them. I stood back once I got into earshot.

Nygren spoke with a high voice that seemed too young for a man with salt and pepper hair. "Given the growth in tree roots that surrounds the body, I say it has been down in the ground for about thirty years. Of course, we will need the forensic experts in Bismarck to determine that."

Bruce stood up. He was a portly man with sideburns and a handlebar mustache that wasn't even fashionable in the seventies. "Do you think it was a child?"

"We can't jump to the conclusion without the state's examination," Nygren explained. "Of course, it is disturbing that the skeleton is wearing a Boy Scout belt. Now, I proudly made it all the way to Eagle Scout, but I stop wearing my buckle when I went off to college. I'm sorry, Bruce, but I have to call the State police in."

"You do what you have to do," Stiejim replied gruffly.

Nygren and Stiejim rose. Nygren caught a glance at me and waved. Stiejim turned at me sternly and then looked away. He remained by the hole as Nygren walked over to me.

"Hi there, Mrs. Mulroney," he greeted warmly, shaking my hand. "Quite a discovery you made today."

I felt comfortable with Sherriff Nygren. I met him a couple of times last year when I taught his son, Caleb.

"That is an understatement, Sherriff Nygren," I said with a weak smile.

"Well, this is what has to happen," Nygren explained, "I'll need to call in the forensic unit from Bismarck. It is going to take two hours for them to get here. As I was telling Chief Stiejim, the cadaver has been buried in your yard for a few decades based on the growth of the tree root surrounding it," he pointed to the woods that separate my yard from Valley City State University campus.

"Since part of the cadaver is exposed to the elements, the forensic team will need to work to extract the body from the ground to completion. It is forecast to snow tonight, and we can't risk moisture damaging the remaining tissue the forensic team has to work with. It will be hours. Unfortunately, it being winter, we don't have a place to occupy kids indoors. I suggest you take your family over to Fargo.

There's an indoor playground at the mall.

"My family went to Fargo yesterday."

"Well, I don't know if it is wise for your children to be around when the cadaver is dug up," Nygren said sincerely, "kids tend to get freaked out about the commotion. Heck, I am a little freaked about the situation. A family is going to receive a gruesome Christmas present this year."

I gave Nygren an understanding nod before turning to my house. From the corner of my eye, I caught Holly Schuler and her older sister standing on their backyard deck dressed in their church clothes. They must have seen the police cars in my driveway when they came home.

"Is everything all right, Mrs. Mulroney?" Holly shouted.

"Just fine, Holly!" I called back.

Mrs. Schuler stuck her head out the window. I waved. She waved awkwardly and motioned her daughters to come back inside. I proceeded to my house as I heard heavy steps crunching snow behind me.

"Mrs. Mulroney, I'll need to ask you a couple of questions," Stiejim announced.

"Sure," I stammered.

I held the door for him. Tim stood in the kitchen, drinking beer. He handed an unopened bottle to Stiejim, who waved it away.

"I'm on duty," he retorted.

Tim smiled his cocky grin. "I am sure that you could make an exception for this brew. This beer is a genuine chocolate porter from Belgium."

Stiejim was a middle age American man, not a naïve college girl who normally fell for Tim's charm. "If I want to drink chocolate, I have an office full of Swizz Miss packets to select from. I also prefer my beer brewed in America, where we don't need to put chocolate in our booze to get people to drink it. Besides, it's not five o'clock yet."

Tim muttered under his breath, "You brew piss water here."

Stiejim sat down at the kitchen table uninvited. Tim and I reluctantly sat on the chairs across from him. Stiejim took out a small notepad from his coat pocket while I took my coat off. Tim stared at Siejim with his arms crossed. He didn't trust a cop he couldn't bribe with a drink.

Stiejim skipped the pleasantries. "Why were the two of you digging in your yard?"

Tim shrugged. "It's our yard."

Stiejim shot him a hard look. "It's not your yard. Your family rents this house. You shouldn't be digging without your landlord's permission. What should go without saying is that people don't dig up their yard in the winter, even if they own the property. What reason did the two of you have to dig in your yard?"

Tim got up from the table. "I don't know, ask Catherine. I need to check on the kids."

Tim left me alone in the kitchen with Stiejim. Since I moved to North Dakota, I quickly learned that men only worked things out amongst each other and women have no choice but to accept it. At this moment I wouldn't have mind the misogynistic paradigm. Tim at least could have acted like a supportive spouse and spoken up for me, using whatever guy language needed to sweep the matter under the rug. Yet, that would be too much to ask of him.

Despite the poorly insulated house, I was sweating. Stiejim arched an eyebrow.

"Well, I saw my son carrying our snow shovel from the window. I caught him just as he was attempting to break ground, which would have broken the shovel because it is plastic. Anyways, I asked him whatever was he doing, and he told me my Christmas present was underneath the ground."

"So, you dug up your yard because your child told you your Christmas present was in the yard?"

"I allowed my curiosity get the best of me."

Stiejim twisted his mouth then leaned back quietly on his chair. As he stared off into the distance, I felt a pit growing in my stomach. I knew I sounded crazy, yet I half expected Stiejim to quickly dismiss me as a lunatic and go on with his day as I often seen him do when the towns people presented him with banal concerns.

Stiejim got up from his chair, "I am going to have to talk to your son."

Without an invitation, he proceeded up the stairs. I followed him to prevent a possible conflict between him and Tim. Tim had a deep seeded resentment of the police since his juvenile delinquent days in Ireland. He would not be happy that I'd allowed the police to talk to our son. Being there was a body in our yard I felt like I had no choice but to have Stiejim talk to Jacob. The police weren't going to leave our house until they had an explanation.

Thankfully, both Jacob and Tim cooperated when Stiejim requested talk to Jacob alone. Jacob took Stiejim to his room. I remained in my room as Maggie sat on Tim's lap watching cartoons. Tim's ice blue eyes locked on me.

"Catherine, don't you think we ought to call a lawyer before we let the cops interrogate our son?"

I shrugged, "Jacob's six. Stiejim won't be hard on him."

I didn't believe the words I had just said. Tim shot me a knowing glare then went on to pretend to be interested in the Disney cartoon Maggie was watching. I stood with my back against the door jam with my eye closed.

Suddenly I heard knocking inches away from my ear. I opened my eyes and turned my head to see Stiejim standing outside the bedroom.

"Mr. and Mrs. Mulroney, I need to talk to you some more."

Jacob walked back into our bedroom to entertain Maggie. Tim and I followed Stiejim down our stairs back to the kitchen table. We watched his eyes dart to every downstairs window in view from the table. His eyes stopped at the small box window over the sink that Tim managed to insulate.

"You are going need to cover more windows than that tiny one if you want to your house to stay warm. Then again, all that hot tea you British drink must keep you warm."

"Shall I brew some?" I asked.

"I suppose," Stiejim accepted.

Tim and I drank coffee rather tea, yet I always kept a box of English Breakfast tea bags for visitors expecting a cup. I filled three random mugs from the cupboard with water and heated them individually in the microwave.

Stiejim started his questions as I prepared the tea. "What do you know about Jacob's friend, Jake?"

"I've never seen him," Tim answered, "Catherine believes in some psychobabble that Jake is an imaginary friend projected by our son's ideal American self."

"Well," I replied, "Jake is how most American boys named Jacob refer to themselves and he has been taking an interest in American football and hockey which isn't common in Europe. I figured he was trying out his new American identity by claiming him to be a friend."

Stiejim gave me a stern look that I have only seen in the rare moments I saw Uncle Oswald work during a court session-the look I could only classify as "You are insane, and I am going to prove it with my next statement" look.

"So, you decided to dig up your yard based on a statement from your son's imaginary friend?"

I pursed my lips. Stiejim bought my silence as confirmation of my assumed insanity. Stiejim tapped his pencil against the table.

"Jacob said that 'Jake' is a thirteen year old boy who plays hockey. He's given me a description, but he doesn't sound like anyone I know around here."

"What would a thirteen-year-old boy be doing hanging around a six-year-old?" I exclaimed.

"That concerned me," Stiejim said, "along with Jacob mentioning that 'Jake' made references to sodomy, which is not a common phrase for a child of Jacob's age to know."

"Sodomy?" I questioned, "Are you talking about rape?"

"Jacob doesn't even know about sex," Tim commented, "as far as I am aware he believes that angels put Maggie in Catherine's stomach when she got pregnant."

Stiejim got up from the table as I place the tea in front of him. "I'm going back to the station to do some more research. 'Jake' could be from a neighboring town. I'll check recent crime reports."

Stiejim walked out of the house without a "goodbye". Tim and I looked out from the side windows to the front door as he got into his car. As he pulled out, the North Dakota Crime Bureau's van pulled into our street. Nygren directed the team into our backyard.

"What do we do now?" I asked.

"Keep our blinds shut," Tim remarked as he sulked upstairs.

Maggie woke up with gas in the middle of the night. I walked her downstairs and pulled the rocking chair to our picture window that faced the backyard. I always loved the look of winter with the white snow blanketing the earth, reflecting the moon whose shine is no longer shield by tree leaves. I could see the snow-covered steeple of Valley City State University's clock tower. My window resembled a Christmas card until my eyes diverted to the five-foot-long hole in my yard. All I could think was *which lucky family is going to get the news their loved one was buried in my backyard?*

I wondered if Nygren knew I understood what he meant when he mentioned a family was going to get a gruesome gift for Christmas. I waited for that gruesome gift my entire life. My brother's whereabouts, dead or alive, would have been a gift. It was the uncertainties that broke my family apart. Jake was somewhere and nobody knew where to look nor who to call. Even when everyone resolved that Jake died, not knowing at whose hand and why continued our descent into madness.

The moment Jacob was first put into my arms when he was born, I understood why my mother became insane. I couldn't bear it if my son or daughter disappeared. As I rocked Maggie and stared at the hole, the reality hit me. The child in my yard had a mother who longed to rock him again.

Tears rolled down my eyes for that child and his mother. I wondered if Stiejim or Nygren would introduce me to the family of the dead child in my yard. I could at least tell them I understood, somewhat. My thoughts continued to spiral until I fell asleep in the rocking chair thinking, *since I uncovered a gruesome crime, would fate bestow kindness to me by giving me the answer to the crime that haunted me.*

5

After I had put Maggie down, I fell into a restless dream where fancy black cars drove down my street. I awoke as Tim grabbed my foot. "Catherine! I need you to help me with the kids!"

My head started throbbing! In the twenty years we knew each other, Tim learned I got migraines whenever I awoke abruptly. Still, his needs overshadowed his ability to deducing cause and effect. Hell, if the effect wasn't about him, he didn't care.

In a daze of pain, I walked downstairs to find my children in the same state, mashing oatmeal in their mouths. "Are you two okay?"

"We're teething," Jacob answered.

"Teething?" I asked.

"Maggie's getting, and I'm losing."

Tim walked into the kitchen wearing his overcoat. He grabbed his scarf off the coat rack. "I'm going to work."

"What! The University is out for winter break!"

"True, and I have to post auditions notices the moment the students get back. I haven't selected a play yet." Then he pointed to a sticky note on the refrigerator. "Oh, Captain Stiejim called. He wants to meet with you. I told him you would meet with him at noon."

I glanced at the kitchen clock. It was 10:45 am. I had an hour and fifteen minutes to shower, dress, dress the kids and walk them to the police station because Tim just grabbed the keys to our one car for a trip where he could simply walk across our backyard onto campus. Knowing that he left me in a bind, he bent down and gave me a kiss.

"I made coffee," he said.

As if I would have the time to drink it.

Somehow, I showered, dressed myself and the children, and had them on the sled to tow them to the Valley City Police Department at 11:45am. Forgoing makeup, jewelry, and styling my hair beyond blow drying shaved time. I was a married woman who was not attracted to anyone at the police department, getting gusty up was unnecessary. I just threw on jeans, a fleece top, and my sneakers. With the children, I just grabbed the first thing in their drawers.

The weather was pleasant. The gray skies insulated the city. We could bear a fifteen-minute walk properly bundled. The children always preferred being pulled on the sled instead of driving during the winter. I found it to be a great upper body workout as I pulled them through the snowy sidewalks. Jacob and Maggie giggled the entire sled ride. Listening to my children's joyful laughter lighten my foul mood.

My lighten mood was short lived. Stiejim was waiting with his arms across his chest at the entrance as the kids, and I walked through the door at a minute afternoon. His eyes darted on the long plastic sled I towed the kids in.

"Tim took our car to work," I explained.

"I see," he said. "At least you don't have to strap the kids in that as you do a car; however, I don't see where you are going to be able to store that thing as we talk."

I propped the sled against the wall. "Would right here be okay?"

Stiejim raised his eyebrows, "I suppose."

The kids and I followed Stiejim through the door to the side of the building that housed the Valley City Police Department. We passed the desk of the open floor plan until we reached Stiejim's private office. He shut the door behind us as I situated the kids with their video games and coloring books on the floor. Stiejim motioned me to take the chair in front of his desk. As I sat down, he placed a manila folder on his desk in front of me.

"The preliminary report has come from Bismarck. The information I received prompted me to dig up more information on you."

My heart froze in my chest. Stiejim was insinuating that he had done a background check. Tim and I each had an arrest on our record. When we were twenty, we walked around London after our Christmas celebration with Marguerite. On a drunken lark, we decided to peek into people's windows to observe how they were celebrating Christmas. As we looked in, we made up stories of hidden dysfunctions of the seemingly functional families. We'd invent stories of the mother having a pill addiction because her husband was having an affair with a transvestite and other silly things of the like. One family caught us and called the police. We weren't charged with anything. Scotland Yard pitied us as the pathetic lot we were and send us off on our way. Then again, that crime wouldn't reach an American database.

"You're not English," he remarked.

"I never said I was," I answered. "That is just an assumption people made because I moved here from England with the accent. You are right; I wasn't born in England."

"You weren't born too far from here, only the next state over," Stiejim commented, "In Stillwater, Minnesota."

"Yes," I confirmed.

"Being from Stillwater, you must have heard about the disappearance of Jake Rhinelander."

I felt the popped in my brain as my mind went blank when Stiejim mentioned my brother's name. I had no clue why he would mention my brother until suddenly I realized he must have heard about my rant two days earlier. Stiejim arched his eyebrows to coerce an explanation from me.

"He would have been my older brother," I replied.

"Would have been?"

"He died before I was born."

Stiejim leaned back in his chair. "I read the case. The Rhinelander boy never was found, dead or alive."

"It was the conclusion my family accepted a decade after his disappearance."

"So, I have heard," Stiejim commented, "Did you know that Jake was a Boy Scout?"

"I assumed he was because I knew my other three brothers were."

"As you know there was a Boy Scout belt buckle attached to the corpse you unearthed from your yard. Before the lab analyzed it, they found two numbers engraved on the belt buckle. One was the club number. The other one was the member number. The club number belonged to a Stillwater troop, and the other was the membership number of Jake Rhinelander."

"That can't be," I whispered.

"Imagine my surprise when I looked up family information and discovered his closest relative was you. This sheds a different light on things..."

"Mum, I pulled my tooth out!"

I turned around. Jacob was holding out his bloody molar. "Now the tooth fairy is going to come."

Stiejim reached his hand over to Jacob. "I know of a better place to send a tooth than giving it to the tooth fairy."

"No way!" Jacob yelled, "The tooth fairy will give me a dollar."

Stiejim pulled out a bundle of gift cards from a desk drawer. "Do you like burgers?"

"I like pizza and tacos better," Jacob replied.

Stiejim reached into his back pocket and pulled out his wallet. He presented my son a ten-dollar bill. "If you give me your tooth, I'll give you ten dollars to go to the taco place afterward, sounds good?"

"Good!" Jacob exclaimed.

Stiejim pulled out a plastic bag. Jacob dropped his tooth inside the open bag. Stiejim sealed it. Stiejim smiled at Jacob as he reached into the desk drawer for police badge stickers. He peeled one and stuck it on Jacob's shirt. "Your heroic deed earned you the title of 'Junior Police Deputy.'"

Maggie looked up from her coloring books. "I want a sticker!"

Stiejim handed another sticker to Jacob, "Give this to her," then he turned to me, "You know why I want the tooth?"

I shook my head.

"The tooth has Mitochondrial DNA. That is only passed through the mother and can be found in tooth pulp. Your brothers wouldn't have the same mDNA as their children, but would have the same as your kids."

"I still don't get what you need my son's tooth."

"Well, the belt buckle only clued the police to the corpses' possible identity. Comparing the Mitochondrial DNA from Jacob's tooth to the remaining teeth of the corpse will determine if the dead child is Jake Rhinelander. Now, I have a drive to Bismarck. They close for the holidays in two days. It is best to get the tooth to the forensic police right away."

Stiejim put on his coat and left without a farewell. I hastily bundled the children in their coats and scurried them out of the police station.

The idea of spending the afternoon cooped up with the kids in the house didn't appeal to me. All I'd do was ruminate about Stiejim's theory. I figured to drop in on Tim under the guise that the kids and I were surprising him with lunch. We stopped at the taco shop, although I didn't pay with the money Stiejim gave Jacob. Tooth fairy money should always be for the child to spend frivolously, not to be used to feed the family.

The university was mostly vacant. The children and I walked up three flights of stairs of MacFarland Hall to get to Tim's office. We found Tim at his desk with his eyes glued to his laptop. Unopened scripts covered his desk. Unaware of our presence Tim shouted, "Goal!"

"Nice to see you hard at work," I greeted.

Tim quickly shut his laptop. Maggie and Jacob ran to him, "Daddy!"

"Mo cuishles!" Tim called out.

"The cop gave me money for my tooth, and we bought tacos!" Jacob explained.

"The cop gave you money...."

"I'll explain later," I interrupted.

I got the kids situated with their tacos as Tim walked across the hall to the break room. He came back with two cans of iced tea, two juice boxes, and a baby food tub of squash. Tim kept provisions in the department's refrigerator for when the kids stopped by for a visit. Maggie, who didn't eat tacos, enjoyed dipping the seasoned tater tots in her squash.

Tim opened the wrapper to his taco. "You forgot the lettuce." "No, I didn't," I replied, "I asked to leave the lettuce off the tacos."

Tim groaned, "Some people like lettuce."

"I hate lettuce and I bought the tacos. Deal with it."

"I didn't ask you come," Tim retorted, "I would have been happy peacefully going over my scripts while eating my soup."

"And you were working so hard," I snorted. "How is the play selection coming?"

Tim motioned to the messy stack of scripts. "I found nothing in the VCSU Library but mid-twentieth-century musicals. I checked out a tune from each on YouTube. All I've seen is overly perky songs and dance numbers. Earlier this week, President Vickerson forwarded me a letter she received from some senior citizen who enjoys how the university puts on 'Seven Brides for Seven Brothers' every seven years, this year being the seventh year. It was a preempted thank-you note. I am not picking a play because some old biddy wants to see the same lame musical for the hundredth and final time."

"Why not?" I asked, "It's a good story. I used to watch the film with Grandma Alice all the time."

"This is a university," Tim proclaimed, "People come to universities to be challenged and pushed through art! There is nothing challenging about a sappy musical."

Valley City State University was mainly known as a premiere university for business and technology in North Dakota. The university didn't have an official acting program in their school of Fine Arts. Theatre was an extracurricular activity the students participated in, crossing off "acting" on their bucket list while adding something to their resume.

"Any script caught your fancy?" I asked.

"I have been researching on how the University could obtain the rights to perform 'Equuas.'"

"The play where that kid from 'Harry Potter' showed his wiener? You have to be joking!"

"Weiner?" Jacob exclaimed from the floor, "Mummies shouldn't be saying wiener."

"Yeah, Ketty," Tim joked, "you shouldn't be talking vulgarly in front of the kids."

I looked over at my children. The crummy mess in front of them indicated they were done with their food. "Jacob, why don't you take Maggie to the rehearsal room," I suggested.

"And do what?" he asked.

"Play."

Jacob took Maggie's hand and walked her over to the room next to us. Tim and I left the door open to hear them. I quickly threw away the children's trash as Tim chuckled, "You kicked the kids out to continue your talk about 'wieners'?"

"I was at the police station," I remarked, "Aren't you going to ask me how my interrogation went?"

"Ah yes, that," Tim replied, "how is our lovely friend, Cheif Stiejim?"

"As suspicious as ever," I answered, "especially since the police think the body found in our backyard is Jake."

"As in Jacob's friend?"

"As in my brother."

"The one who was kidnapped? Impossible."

"Stiejim told me the Boy Scout belt buckle found on the corpse had numbers engraved on the back. The member number and troop number belonged to Jake Rhinelander of Stillwater, Minnesota. Stiejim started looking for relatives. He found me."

"How did he find you? Your name isn't Rhinelander anymore."

"My social security number is still same. They probably found me through that and traced me to Valley City because I work in town. Stiejim mentioned he was looking for the nearest relative. He wasn't searching for me per se."

Tim leaned back in his chair tapping a pen against his knuckles. "This is all occurring right after you ranted in front of your students about Jake. All of this is a joke. Your students are playing a prank on you."

"How can you be saying that?"

"Students love to pull pranks on the teacher. We did."

True, Tim and I pulled a prank on Mrs. Drinkwater in eleventh grade. That is because she ridiculed our friend, Patrick, who stuttered whenever she asked him a question. We bought curries from an Indian market and slipped it into her tea. Still, I never humiliated a student based on disabilities.

"I've given my students no cause to play a prank like that."

"You never know what your students are thinking," Tim said, "Mrs. Drinkwater thought we believed she was helping Patrick when she mimicked him."

"The only likely student I humiliated was the Schuler girl. She apologized to me for her own doing yesterday!"

"A dead body is found in our yard, and it's your brother? Get with it, Ketty. It's impossible."

I didn't know what to believe. Before yesterday, I thought it was impossible that a dead body was buried in my yard. Now I found myself being hit with a bunch of information with little time to process it. I found Tim's ability to drum up basic answers annoying.

Tim turned his computer screen my direction with a map of the United States uploaded.

"This is how jurisdictions work," Tim said. "Each state is its own jurisdiction. The cops can only make an arrest within their state borders."

"That's the basics," I replied, surprised my husband somehow took the time to learn about United States laws.

Tim pointed to the border of Minnesota and Wisconsin. "This is Stillwater. The next town east to it is Houlton, Wisconsin. The kidnappers most likely would go to Wisconsin to avoid being in Minnesota jurisdiction for a lengthy amount of time. To go to Valley City from Stillwater, the creep who kidnapped your brother would have to drive across the entire state of Minnesota to get to North Dakota. If the kidnapper was going to risk remaining in Minnesota for a lengthy about of time, the most logical direction would be north into Canada, outside of any Federal jurisdiction."

Tim's explanation made sense, but it was too simplistic to rule out the possibility entirely that Jake was taken into North Dakota. "Police don't pull a person over for having a child in his car."

Tim shrugged, "True, but the possibility of the body being your brother is more wishful thinking than anything."

We heard a crash from the rehearsal room. Both of us ran in to find Jacob in a tangled mess of chairs and music stands. Maggie cried at the calamity. Tim went to comfort Maggie as I went help Jacob. Footsteps approached us. "Hello, Nancy," Tim greeted.

Nancy Cartwright, President Vickerson's secretary, stood in the doorway. "Everything all right?" she asked, "I heard the crash from my office."

"Just kids being kids," I answered.

"I see," she replied. "Well, I am going to out. Maintenance will want to be locking up the building early since the school is out. Are you going to be long? If not, I'll walk out with you all."

"We are done," I answered, "if fact, Tim was going to email President Vickerson that he selected 'Seven Brides for Seven Brothers' to be the winter community play."

"Oh, that will be lovely," Nancy said. "Tim has been incredible at getting internationally acclaimed musical acts for our community; however, I am glad that we are sticking to traditional fare for the theatrical performances. I will be shutting down my office. Come and get me after you get the kids ready."

Nancy left. I went to gather the kids' winter clothes. Tim grabbed Maggie's coat when I returned to the rehearsal room. "On what authority did you have to select the University's production?"

"On the authority as your wife," I said as I put Maggie's hat on her head, "It is my right to invoke when you are about to make a stupid decision. People in this state love their horses, but will not appreciate the way Alan Strang loved them. We'd be run out of town if you selected 'Equus'."

"As if we aren't at risk of that given that the town knows there was a body buried in our yard," Tim snorted.

Tim always had a way of making situations harder than they ought to be with his unnecessary comments. I knew that the town probably knew about yesterday's gruesome discovery when I noticed the Schuler girls witnessing the ordeal. Still, Tim didn't need to use the situation as a retort.

Dressed in our winter clothes, we went to the first floor to Nancy's office. She shut down her computer. The door adjacent to her desk was locked. President Vickerson wasn't in. When she was, the kids knew they needed to be quiet. In her absence, the children took whatever liberties they could. Maggie immediately crawled over to the shelf connected to Nancy's desk to play with her snowmen figurines. Jacob started scribbling on her memo pad. I tried gathering them back to the doorway as fast as I could. Tim only stood in the doorway shooting me looks.

"I am so sorry, Nancy," I apologized while grabbing Maggie.

Nancy put on her coat. "Kids will be kids."

Jacob handed Nancy a piece of paper. "Mrs. Cartwright, can you see that President Vickerson gets my calling card?"

Nancy read the pink message memo, "I will not because your name is not Paddington Fartsworth, Jacob."

Jacob laughed hysterically. Tim and I led the children to the grand entrance of MacFarland Hall, too embarrassed look Nancy in the eye.

Nancy broke the silence as we walked out to the cement steps. "Catherine, how are you doing?"

I knew Nancy had a daughter in the eighth grade; therefore, she at least heard about my ranting about prayers and Jake.

"I am doing okay given the circumstances," I replied.

"Well, don't you worry about fixing a thing for the party; everyone around here will understand you are too busy to cook. Just bring yourselves."

Nancy parted ways once we were near the parking lot. Tim looked over at me expecting me to walk the children home on the sled. In a rare moment that he was cognizance of his solipsistic thinking, he pressed the button on his key fob that opened the truck. He put away the sled while I secured the children in their booster seats.

Once we were all in the car, I asked, "What party was Nancy talking about?"

"Oh, President Vickerson is holding a party on Christmas Day for the faculty members who are in town this holiday without family. As far I know Aunt Rebecca isn't going to be visiting us."

"True, she is visiting her sister in Arizona this year," I answered as we drove down College Street, "How long have you known about this party?"

"Oh, invitations were sent out after Thanksgiving," Tim answered.

"You knew a month ago and didn't think it was pertinent to tell me!"

Tim shrugged, "You know now?"

"Whatever am I to do? The groceries stores will have depleted shelves tomorrow!"

"Nancy gave you an out," Tim replied as he pulled up our driveway, "What the…"

From the car, I saw a multitude of insulated bags containing casserole dishes upon our front step. It was the tradition in North Dakota to give families going through significant ordeals. Tim got out of the car to look at them. "Guess what, Ketty? The hot dish committee has been here. The town loves us!"

That night the children ate a tater-tot hot dish from the Krutesburgs while Tim and I ate the Puerto Rican rice and beans Mia Vellon's mother made. Tim spent the evening upstairs reading the "Seven Brides for Seven Brothers" while I sat with the kids as they watch a marathon of cartoon Christmas Specials. I wrote thank you notes to give to people when I returned their dishes.

My task didn't distract me from the hole in our backyard. Tim kept on insisting that the whole situation was a prank. He wasn't figuring the corpse was three feet deep in the ground. The ground in the yard never shown any evidence of disturbance before my striking the shovel to it.

I started thinking about timelines. Jacob had been talking to Jake since the September he began Kindergarten. I have heard Jacob speaking to him in his room; therefore, I didn't think Jake would be real. Could it be possible for there to be an actual Jake and an imaginary Jake?

Something in my gut knew my son wouldn't have come up with the idea to dig up a body on his own. If "Jake" was truly a real, he was around long before I disclosed to my students about my missing brother.

That night it was my turn to read to Jacob before bed. We started a book from "The Boxcar Children" series. After I finished the first chapter I asked him, "Jacob, how do you know Jake?"

"Jake who?"

"Your friend, Jake."

Jacob quickly stammered, "He's not my friend."

"Why would you say that? You have been talking about hanging around him for a while. It sounds like you were pretty thick with him."

"He's weird. He thought you would want a mummy for Christmas."

"A mummy?"

"Not like you," Jacob answered, "like those bodies in pyramids. You know, like we saw when we went to that museum with Aunt Rebecca. Is that was what was in our yard?"

I sighed. No matter how Jacob appeared immersed in his video games, he picked up on more than I thought.

"No, Jacob, it wasn't the same thing," I said.

"Oh," Jacob said as he turned over in his covers away from me.

I knew Jacob was distressed talking about "Jake". If the situation weren't dire, I'd just let it go and let him sleep. Tonight, I needed to get to the bottom of "Jake's" existence since there was a possibility of someone attempting to prey on my child.

"Jacob, is Jake real?"

Jacob pulled the covers over his head.

"Jacob, it is all right to have imaginary friends…"

Jacob gave a muffled shout, "I wish he were!"

"What do you mean?"

Jacob rolled the covers away from his face. "I mean he can disappear."

"Disappear?"

"And he pops out of nowhere."

"I don't understand."

"Like I was shooting my hockey puck against the garage one day and I wasn't very good. Jake came out of nowhere and told me how to hit it. It was pretty cool. Then he asked me to shoot the puck at him, and I thought he was crazy. Then I shot it at him and it went through him!"

"Oh my god!"

"Yeah, it was pretty cool."

"How so?"

"Because it was, Mum," Jacob said exasperated. "Why are you asking so many questions about Jake?"

"He's been your friend for a while and I don't know him," I answered.

"Yes, you do."

"I really don't."

"Jake told me you know him! He says you two are really close."

"I don't know a…"

The temperature dropped ten degrees. Suddenly the light began to flicker until it went out. Jacob burrowed his entire being underneath the covers. I heard his muffled voice, "He's here."

My eyes darted around the room. I saw nothing. The feeling of heavy static charged the atmosphere. The house was over a century old. I knew that. Still, the faulty wiring and the old heater never produced a dramatic outage.

"Do you want to sleep in Mummy and Daddy's room?"

Jacob peeked from the covers, "Can I?"

I carried Jacob to my room. He was a solid kid despite his lanky appearance. I practically dropped him on my bed. Jacob scurried to the middle and burrowed himself into the mattress. Tim walked into the bedroom from Maggie's room.

"What's Jacob doing in here?"

"He's sleeping here."

"Why?"

"Because he is," I remarked slashing the air with my hand. I didn't feel like giving Tim reasons he'd only discredit. I tired of his blasé attitude at times. Even if what happened in Jacob's room was just our imaginations getting the best of us, the past two days defined reasoning. Tim retreated from questioning me further. I grabbed my shirt and yoga pants to dress in the bathroom.

I walked out of the bathroom after I readied for bed. Tim had closed the bedroom door. I hear his voice filtering out. The hall light was off, but I could see my way. I turned to my right.

The light came from Jacob's room.

6

Jacob hadn't slept in my bed since he was a baby. Thankfully, he still slept like one, quiet and still. I didn't sleep as peacefully as the boy cuddled next to me. My dream disturbed my rest.

I walk into my house to find three children sitting on random furniture in the lower level. They turn to look at me somberly as I walk through the kitchen to the living room. They are translucent. Suddenly, I feel pressure from my back that bubbles through my abdomen. Jacob emerges through my being and proceeds up the steps unaware of the other beings around him. I hear my voice from the front door calling out, "Jacob, don't run in the house."

I turn to the door. I see myself pregnant with Maggie at the doorway. Tim is closely behind carrying our rucksacks. I turn at the disappointed faces of the three children. A girl braiding strands of her long dark hair sat near the living room window. The boy faces me from the sofa where the ghost of a nineteen eighties He-Man episode is playing on the television behind him. I turned to a light hair girl wearing nineteen seventies clothing sitting at the kitchen table. In a voice devoid of life she utters, "You came back. Why would you do that?"

Maggie's crying woke me up. She pooped during the night. It squished out of her diaper and pushed up across her back. I took her to the bathroom and into the shower with me. Holding Maggie, I turned on the faucet and allowed the warm water to hit my face. Maggie nuzzled her face in my neck. We stood under the shower head until the water turned cold.

I looked the clock in the bathroom. Since it was before dawn, I put Maggie in another sleeper thinking she would be settling down again. Instead she wanted to play. I took her downstairs so she wouldn't disturb Jacob and Tim from sleeping. Her happy squeals woke up Jacob. He came downstairs and occupied Maggie while I made them eggs for breakfast. He entertained Maggie with his own rendition of "Down by the Bay".

"Did you ever see a bear, combing his hair? He's the one wearing poopy underwear. I like to fart!"

Maggie giggled uncontrollably. I knew I ought to scold Jacob for using potty language; however, taking cherished songs and making their lyrics dirty had always been a timeless part of childhood. I found relief in Jacob's ability to interact with his sister in a silly manner as an indication that he had forgotten the strange occurrences the night before.

"I like to fart and name it Bart. Fart, fart, fart, fart. Fart, fart, fart, fart."

Tim didn't share Maggie's amusement to Jacob's transposition.

"Wow that is poetic and noetic all at the same time."

"Be nice," I grumbled as he passed me to get to the cupboard where we kept the coffee mugs.

"He's being idiotic," Tim replied.

I rolled my eyes. When it came to parenting, Tim was a hypocrite. Not too long-ago Tim was an idiotic child. He behaved less appropriately than Jacob ever had.

"They are just being children," I said. "Maggie is enjoying the song, so let them be."

Tim stares at Maggie then shrugged, "Maggie would laugh at the news the world was going to end if you presented it with enough enthusiasm."

After a night of restless sleep, I didn't want to be around Tim's irritable morning mood. When the kids were done with breakfast, I snuck upstairs to dress.

"I'm going to be out for a few minutes," I announced as I walked to the coat rack.

Tim turned from the living room couch stunned. "Where do you have to go?"

"To the store," I answered, "I need to get something for the Christmas party."

"We got tons of food here!"

"I think it is against Midwestern protocol to regift hot dishes," I said, "besides, I have to go to the school as well. There were a few things I forgot to complete before it let out for Christmas break."

"You can't leave me with the kids! I have work to do."

I stared at the soccer game on Tim's tablet computer. He did work hard on keeping up with the Manchester United Futbol club. Too bad for him I didn't considered it to be an admirable effort.

"Maggie ought to be going down for an early nap. She's been awake since four this morning. Jacob is well trained in keeping himself busy as you focus on your futbol. You'll have a quiet afternoon."

I bundled into my winter gear and walked out the door. The cold air motivated me to snap out of my sluggishness and move quickly. Reaching a warm destination wasn't my only objective. I had a fact finding mission to complete.

The building to Valley City Senior and Junior High School was open. Maintenance workers and administrators still had work to complete during the holiday break. A couple of other teachers were known for coming in to grade students' assignments in peace. I passed the administration office catching a snippet of a conversation.

"She is not really English?"

I had stopped before I passed the open door. I recognized the voice belonging to Sarah Oakes, the high school music teacher. I often found her gossiping to her best friend Kara Sorenson in the head administrator's office.

"Nope," Kara answered, "her birth certificate is from Minnesota."

"Then why does she talk like she is British?"

"Her degrees are from England. I knew she was American. My niece, Paige, was in her son's kindergarten class. I think he mentioned to her that his mum and dad married so his dad could enter the United States."

"He's English?"

"No, he's Irish," I spoke.

Kara and Sarah turned to find me standing in the doorway.

"My son was also born in Ireland," I continued, "and you can go to Mercy Hospital's Nursery online scrapbook to verify that my daughter was born here in Valley City. Any other questions you have?"

"Uh no," Sarah answered perturbed that I had the gull to confront them.

"Very well," I said, "carry on with your gossiping. I heard a rumor that there are people living in this town that were born in Canada."

"Yeah," Kara answered, "the Nortons are from Winnipeg,"

"Gosh, before we know it, Valley City is going to be overtaken by all those pesky foreigners," I joked.

I turned away and proceeded to my office. Luckily, the third floor to the Junior high section was empty so I escaped run-ins with other gossipy folks. I entered my classroom; no one else heard the door click echo through the halls as it shut behind me.

I logged into my computer to the school's intranet to pull up this year's roster. I taught the entire seventh grade body English. My students were the age that my son's "friend", Jake. I never knew of a Jake in my class. My students were born in the era when parents gave their sons last names as first names. I stared at the roster reading all the Carsons, Connors, and Jacksons not finding a Jake or a Jacob. I alphabetized middle name knowing sometimes people didn't refer themselves by their first name. All I saw were James, Andrew, and old Scandinavian names such as Anders and Sven. Still didn't see a Jacob or Jake on the list.

Then it hit me. Quite possibly this "Jake" was a sixth grader who turned thirteen after Labor Day. I emailed Diane Hokenson, my predecessor who now was the principal of Washington Elementary. She had the sixth-grade roster. I quickly typed an email asking if she could disclose whether there was a sixth-grade student named Jake or Jacob.

As I shut down my computer, the amount of light decreased. I turned to my left and noticed shadows against the frosted glass of the classroom door. Murmurs floated into the room through the cracks. Expecting Kara and Sarah, I slowly approached so I could covertly listen in without them noticing.

Instead I heard a younger voice, "Do you think she is in there?"

I opened the door to find Holly Schuler, Amy Tinklebaum, Mia Vellon, Trent Lockman, and Leif Wilson along with a dark-haired girl I didn't recognized.

I opened the door. "School's out for the holiday. Didn't you all get the memo?"

Holly stepped slightly forward with an air of importance. "Hello, Mrs. Mulrooney. We hope that you don't mind our visit."

"I don't," I said, "I'm just surprised students would wish to visit their teachers when school out, or that this would be the first place you'd visit."

"It's not," Leif answered. "Holly had us go to your house first. Your husband said you'd be here or at the store."

"I have friends who bag at both grocery stores," Trent continued, "Nobody saw you at either one."

"Well, I am curious to hear what was so important that all of you felt the need to track me down," I commented.

Holly inched forward to me with her arms akimbo, "Prayer works. After this weekend you cannot deny that."

"I'm afraid I don't understand," I replied.

"You said that you gave up prayer because God never told you what happened to your brother. Well, we all prayed for you on Sunday. Then that night, the police were in your yard digging up your brother. Now you know!"

"True," I said, "There was a corpse discovered in my yard; however, it is only speculation that it is my brother. As far as I know, that suspicion hasn't been made public."

"Amy's going out with Caleb Nygren," Trent mentioned.

"Don't tell my parents!" Amy exclaimed.

"Don't worry, Amy. Contrary to popular opinion, teachers don't snitch on their students regarding personal matters unless an incident is life threatening. In your case, it is not."

With that, I noticed Mia slipping her hand into Leif's.

"So, all of you go to the same church?"

"Nope," answered Leif, "Mia is Catholic, I am Lutheran, Trent is also Lutheran but doesn't go to my church. Holly and Amy go to the same nondenominational church."

"Spankey prayed at her church too!" exclaimed the girl I didn't recognized.

Mia sighed, "I apologize, Mrs. Mulroney. This is Spankey Anderson. She followed us when we were picking up Trent."

"My church still prayed. If you all were going to make a big announcement to the teacher, Spankey should be here representing the Episcopalians."

"I am pleased to meet you, Spankey," I said. "I thank you for your prayers. I thank all of you."

Holly shook her head. "Mrs. Mulroney, you do not understand the scope of the situation. We only represent about five percent of the churches that prayed for you and your brother."

"You are saying that the entire town prayed for Jake?"

"Well, we were more realistic," Leif answered, "we prayed that you would learn about what happened to your brother and find peace. But, yeah the entire town prayed."

"Plus, my grandma's church in Minneapolis, my other grandma's church in Madison and her sister's church in Puerto Rico,"

Mia added.

"How is that possible?" I asked.

"I talked to my grandparents," Mia answered.

"And we tweet on Twitter and post on Facebook," Amy commented.

"Spankey is a member of Prayer Group.org," she chimed.

"As am I," Holly said, "this prayer went global."

I stood in front of my students aghast. My belief in prayer may not have been magically alter; however, the students' deed deeply touched me. Any teacher of the seventh grade would be so lucky if one of his/her students cared enough to pray for them. I knew I ought not to be the subjects of any prayers of the six students standing in front of me had bestowed. Leif had a grandmother in hospice care due to cancer. Mia's cousin in Wisconsin had mental illness and the medicine balancing the chemicals in her brain was causing internal bleeding. Amy's brother still struggled with the injuries he sustained while serving in Afghanistan. Trent's family lived near the town's trailer park and I've overheard him talking about a few incidents where the meth related crimes spilled into his backyard. Clearly, they took Jake's story to heart. I became ashamed thinking about how many times I questioned that my students listen. Not only were they listening, they were sharing my brother's story to everyone they cared about.

"Do you kids still like pizza?" I asked.

"This is America," Amy remarked.

I motioned the students to follow me. Bewildered, they allowed me to lead them two flights of stairs to room sparsely furnished with old couches and wooden table and chairs.

"Where are we?" asked Trent.

"The teacher's lounge," I answered, "don't tell anyone I let you in here."

Of course, the teacher lounge wasn't a place of fantasy but it did have a pizza oven. A member of the faculty was related to the owners of Pizza Corner. The faculty freezer was always stocked with their pizza. If a teacher wanted one, all we needed to do put five dollars in a lock box. The students sat around on the couches flipping through dated magazines and Cabelas catalogs while I cooked the pizza. Everyone got to pick a can of pop in the vending machine. When the pizza was done, the students moved to the tabled. I sat nervously. Normally when I sat in front of my students I had a curriculum to dictate the course of discussion. Wanting to forget my own adolescence I lost my ability to talk to teenagers casually.

Then again, Holly Schuler could always jump start any conversation. "So, have you found peace, Mrs. Mulroney?"

"Peace is a process, Holly. However, the first step to peace is knowing that someone cares about your woes. That is what your prayers have shown me. "

"Mrs. Mulroney," Trent asked, "If I ask you a question do you promise not to get mad?"

I took a long sip of my soda. "In my experience, that phrase has never been the proper way to start a question. But yes, you have my word that I will not get mad at your question."

"Why did your parents quit looking?"

I uttered that question in my head multiple times during my adolescence. One night it plagued me terribly that I ended up at the computer lab on campus and typed that question on my search engine. I discovered you couldn't find everything on the internet. As I matured, I formulated an answer I could live with.

"The problem with kidnapping, Trent, is that the kidnapper has the advantage. Whoever kidnapped my brother could cover his tracks before my parents realized Jake was missing. From what I understood, the only evidence was the testimony of my other brothers. Without hard evidence the police didn't know where to look. My family lived near the border of Minnesota and Wisconsin. The police focused more on that area for it seemed logical at the time."

"My mother actually remembers the cops looking for your brother in Wisconsin," Mia said. "It happened the same year her family moved there from Puerto Rico."

"If they couldn't find him in Wisconsin, then why didn't the police look in North Dakota?" Amy asked.

I said what I hoped was true, "My parents looked wherever there were leads. Unfortunately, there weren't many. Being unable to know where Jake was sickened them. They fell into severe depression and..."

Mia hastily interrupted with, "Depression. Enough said."

I heard footsteps behind me. I nearly panic as I turned my head to the door expecting to see Kara, who would snitch me out to the other teacher for giving students access into our meager sanctum. To my surprise, it was Tim standing at the doorway with our kids. Tim's face didn't warrant that he was happy to be seeing me.

I excused myself from the table. Tim's face hardened as I approached. Maggie was still in her pajamas. Jacob looked like he hastily dressed. He saw pizza and headed towards the table.

"What's going on?" I asked taking a sleepy Maggie from Tim's arms.

"I just spent an hour at the police station while you are shooting the breeze with a bunch of kids!"

"The police station?"

"Our buddy, Chief Stiejim, called. He wanted to talk to you and Jacob. I told him you weren't home but he insisted that I still bring Jacob. I've been trying to get a hold of you for a bloody hour!"

I looked at my phone. I had the habit of turning it off whenever I entered the classroom. Sure enough, I subconsciously switched it to silent.

"Stiejim still wants to talk to you," Tim said.

"Are you here to hull me off to the station?"

"No. I had enough of the place. I just came to find you pissing around..."

"Watch your language in front of my students!"

"It's okay, Mrs. Mulroney," Mia said, "We all need to leave."

The students started to gather the paper towels used to placed their pizza slices upon and threw them in the trash. They uttered quick murmurs of gratitude about the pizza as they passed the door. The same awkwardness that clung to the air on the day I ranted about my disbelief in prayer hover over them.

The moment my students were no longer visible, I thrust Maggie into Tim's arms. "If I ever behave like that in front of your students, you would never forgive me."

"I work at the University..."

"You behaved like an arse! That is no excuse!"

"Mummy?" Jacob uttered with a sob in his throat.

I gave Jacob a quick hug and told him I love him before I headed to my classroom for my hat and mittens. Tim didn't linger in the lounge. He gathered the kids and left. Had he behaved properly I may have held some sympathy. He reacted to everything this weekend with his typical self-absorb mannerisms. My students offered me the first real source of comfort through the ordeal. He chased them away!

I walked outside the school and headed west towards Second Street. The biting cold only worsened my mood. If Stiejim wanted to pick another fight like he did the day before, I was ready.

7

Stiejim was smoking by the doorway when I approached the station. He quickly stubbed his cigarette out when he saw me. Without a greeting, he held the door out for me. Once we were inside the building, he bypassed me to appear he was leading me to his office. We took our seats at his desk.

"So, Tim found you."

"Yes, I told him I was at the school."

"Isn't school out?"

"I had research to do. I don't know why Tim couldn't get a hold me. My students were able to track me."

Stiejim looked up at me, "Why were your students looking for you?"

"To inform me that they started a prayer chain at their churches," I answered, "They hoped I would find the answers to my brother's disappearance and find peace."

"Yes, I know. I go to church," Stiejim gruffed as he pulled out an envelope from the case file. "The answer came in today from Bismarck. Your son's mDNA is a perfect match to the corpse. Given the other evidence found on the body, its identity has been determined to be Jacob Allen Rhinelander."

There it was: the answer I always yet never wanted. Stiejim's confirmation vacuumed all the uncertain air that had surrounded my being, creating an empty clarity. I drew a shallow breath in an attempt to remain cognizance of where I sat. Stiejim wasn't about to let me have a moment to digest the news entirely.

Stiejim tapped his pen on his desk. "Now, you know that bodies don't appear because people prayed."

"I know," I sighed.

"Now, one thing I have trouble grappling is why you decided to dig up your yard in the middle of winter."

Stiejim eyed me to replied. "I didn't decide to dig in my yard. It was my son's idea."

"But it wasn't your son who had the idea. He got it from his friend, 'Jake'".

Stiejim slid two pieces of paper across his desk to me. One was my brother's missing person poster. Another was a drawing of him.

Stiejim pointed to the composite sketch. "We had your son, Jacob, in here earlier. One of the art students at the university has a real knack for drawing an accurate portrait of a person just by verbal instructions. She drew this as I asked Jacob questions about his so-called friend. Does he remind you of anyone?"

I picked up both pieces of paper. The poster had my brother's last school picture. He looked forward smiling a goofy wide mouth grin. The composite showed a glum boy with a stern face, but it was undoubtedly the same kid on the poster.

"When did you move to England?"

I peered from between the pages in my hands. "When I was fourteen, why?"

Stiejim shrugged. "I was wondering. So, you lived in Minnesota for fourteen years, moved to England, then moved here to Valley City about two years ago?"

"Almost."

"You had no connections to Valley City when you moved here?"

"Nope. We moved here because of Tim's job."

Stiejim leaned his chair to the left. "It's very unusual that someone moves here from Europe. Not too many people in the United States know of Valley City, North Dakota. I find it strange that someone from a continent that doesn't even know of the state of North Dakota finds a job in Valley City."

"Tim wanted a job as an art director or coordinator. If we had stayed in London, he'd be a lowly intern or an administrative assistant. He applied all over the world. Valley City was the best fit for us."

"Ms. Rhinelander..."

"Mrs. Mulroney," I corrected.

"Catherine, then," Stiejim snided, "I know a little more than about your family than you think I do. For one, I know that you are not the first Rhinelander to enter Valley City's city limits."

"Considering that my brother's body was buried in this town before I was born, I dare say you are right."

Stiejim slid another piece of paper to me. "I meant willingly."

Printed on a piece of paper was a black and white photograph of a man with stringy, greasy light colored hair with patchy facial hair. Below the photo, I saw the name Joseph Allen Rhinelander.

"Look familiar?" Stiejim gruffed.

"Only because he resembles how my father looked the last time I saw him."

"When did you last see your dad?"

"When I was thirteen."

"That's quite a while," Stiejim commented. "It explains some things. What about your brother, Joe? When did you last see him?"

"When I was four?" I guessed.

"When you were four? You know that Joe was in Valley City about a year ago?"

I shook my head.

"He was one of the people I arrested in the big meth bust."

"I don't do drugs."

"After I arrested him he claimed that he saw his brother's spirit. He started going off on how the killer lived here in Valley City. He was such a ranting lunatic that when I hauled him off to Jamestown, I didn't put him in the state pen. I committed him to the state hospital."

Stiejim gave me the evil eye. I didn't have a response to it. It was very possible Joe and I crossed path when he was in Valley City and not know it. I could easily tell him that, but it would be fruitless. In Stiejim's mind, my relation to a drugged out head case alone was a necessary cause for suspicion, furthering his cause in placing blame on the foreigner.

"I've reviewed Joe's file," Stiejim continued, "mental illness and addiction run in your family. Your mother was committed multiple times and your father's dealt with substance abuse."

"My mother lost her son! Of course, that drove her to insanity!"

Stiejim shook his head. This time, he slammed an envelope in front of me. With his silent urging, I open the envelope. The first piece of paper had the insignia of St. Francis Mental Hospital.

Patient Name: Judith Catherine Rhinelander
Admittance Date: July 15th, 1969

"That was long before Jake's disappearance," Stiejim commented.

"Where did you get this?"

"The state hospital sent them over. Apparently, your mother volunteered her information if it helped your brother. There is an admittance record from nineteen seventy as well."

I pulled the pile of paper from the envelope. I flipped through them until I found the intake papers from nineteen seventy. It listed her as the mother of all four of my brothers and their ages. Nick listed as being three months. I flipped back to the first intake paper I saw. Only three of my brothers were listed, Joe being only four months old at the time of my mother's admittance.

Stiejim glared at me, "What does all of it tell you?"

"My mother must have suffered from post-partum depression."

Stiejim snorted. Of course, he'd think postpartum depression as a made up disease because it only affected women.

"Well, your mother isn't the only one in your family that is crazy. Joe has been institutionalized, and there is the matter of your son..."

"What about my son?!"

Stiejim moved his chair back with wide eyes. One of his officers passing by stopped and looked at me through the office window. The buzz from the halogen lights was all that could be heard in the office.

Stiejim glared at me. "It would be best, Ms. Mulroney, if you keep it down. You have enough of the town's attention on you. As you quickly learned when you moved here that it is not always the best thing."

I clenched my jaw. Stiejim had a way of making my blood boil. This time I felt the veins on the verge of bursting. There was no reason Stiejim had dragging my mother's and Joe's mental health records into the public eye just because they were related to the dead body found in my yard.

"Now I have two theories to look into: One being that your son has some inherited mental illness. I have found a child psychologist who will test him tomorrow..."

"Tomorrow? This is impossible..."

"I thought so myself," Stiejim interjected, "but the FBI was able to find a guy willing to work on Christmas Eve given the severity of the case."

"The FBI?"

"We got a case of a boy kidnapped in Minnesota with his body found in North Dakota. Being that two state jurisdictions are involved, it's the FBI's case."

"Then why are you questioning me, not them?"

"Because the FBI has limited manpower," Stiejim answered, "they are involved in most Federal cases concerning children. However, the child is dead. There is no need to pull agents from cases where there is a chance the child is alive. The Valley City Police department is using our men and the FBI will assist us in providing the resources we need. Any more benign questions, Ms. Mulroney, or can we get to business? I need to go over the arrangements that are being made regarding your family."

"What arrangements need to be made?" I asked. "I know my son is not crazy and I am certainly not going to have him endure psychological testing on Christmas Eve which happens to be his birthday!"

"You will do what we tell you to do, Ms. Mulroney!" Stiejim barked.

The entire office fell silent again. Stiejim gave me an accusing glare as he recovered from his outburst. "Your son is going to be tested tomorrow, Ms. Mulroney, or you and your husband will be charged with interfering with a police investigation. Unless you have a confession you would like to make."

"What confession would I have to make?"

"The second theory I have to look into Ms. Mulroney is that your family is responsible for the disappearance."

"You have to be kidding me?"

"Ms. Mulroney, you do realize that the fact you decided to randomly dig in your backyard in the middle of December and found the body identified as your own brother is cause for suspicion. Now, Joe is back in Jamestown again. He was arrested up in Bloom for drug possession. He's in the prison this time. Even now, he rants about see your dead brother's ghost. This time he was saying that the truth was going to be revealed. He drove westward on to Interstate Ninety-Four to get to Bloom. That meant he passed Valley City."

"So he did," I replied, "but that has nothing to do with me or my family!"

"Then tell me what reason you had to dig in your backyard in December!"

I couldn't tell Stiejim that. Instinct and spiritual forces compelling my arms to dig that day would only sound like cop outs to the ears of the man who clearly had it out to me.

"I don't understand this focus on me," I mentioned. "I wasn't even alive when Jake got kidnapped. Joe was nine when it had happened! He had nothing to do with it. If anybody had anything to do with Jake's death, then it was whoever lived in my house when he was kidnapped! Have you dug anything on that person?!"

"The owner of your property is a kind, pious woman named Gladys Han. Everyone in town knows her. I suggest you not be going around town asking about her. It would only make you look guilty."

I had enough of Stiejim. He wasn't going to look into any other theories besides my family being crazy. I needed to get out of there. Simply storming out of the station would only give Stiejim ample reason of my guilt. I took out my smart phone and snapped a picture of myself. Then I threw it down at Stiejim's desk.

"Take this to your contact in Jamestown and show it to Joe. He's not going to recognize me. In fact, find every one of my living brothers. Hell! Find my parents! No one is going to recognized me. I haven't seen my family in seventeen years. It's been a hell of a lot longer since I saw Joe! In fact, I don't have memory of it."

Focused solely on the station's exit sign, I walked out of Stiejim's office.

It was only nineteen degrees outside, too cold for a walk across town.
Thankfully the adrenaline boiled my blood hot enough to brave the walk to my house. The late afternoon Dakota sky was pitch black. The pale moon reflected off the snow illuminating my thoughts as it illuminated the town. Every step away from the police station resulted in a deeper clarity.

Most of the population in Valley City over the age of forty knew everyone in the town for over twenty years or so. As far as I know Stiejim hadn't lived anywhere else. Then there was the way he described the woman who lived in the house, "kind and pious".
Then he warned me not to ask questions about her. Suddenly, Stiejim's motives were clear. He was covering for that Gladys Han!

But why would Stiejim cover for an old lady who used to live in my house? I certainly didn't know him well enough to know which street he lived on. I never heard of him having any relation to anyone in town. Having regular conversations around you get a sense of who is friends with who. No one ever mentioned seeing Stiejim socially.

I walked up my street. My house was dark. Tim didn't think to turn the porch light on for me. The Schuler house shone like a shining beacon with their bushes covered in clear net light.

"Hey, Ms. Mulroney!" I heard behind me.

Holly was walking up the street. She must have been returning from Amy's house. I stood and waited for her.

"Ms. Mulroney, thank you so much for the pizza today," she chattered when she approached. "I found the conversation that we had this afternoon inspiring. I would like to continue it some time for I think that we could learn more from each other."

In Holly speak that meant she thought I could learn from her in the realm of religion. Holly was about to fulfill an opportunity to have my questions answers, just not about religion.

"I do have a question for you, Holly. Have you lived in Valley City all of your life?"

"Nope, I was born in Grand Forks."

"How long have you lived here?"

"Since my dad got the job at John Deer," Holly answered. "I was five when we moved so it would be about eight years."

"So, you knew the people who lived in my house?"

"My parents did."

"Holly, are your parents home?"

8

Holly led me into her house. Her blonde hair cascaded down to her shoulders as she flung off her hat and ran down the hall.

"Mom! Ms. Mulroney is here. She wants to talk to you!"

I hear a couple of hush voices from the entry way. While they talked amongst themselves, I went through the mail laying in a basket by the door. I couldn't remember Holly's parents' names. Holly wasn't my homeroom student; therefore, I didn't have progress conferences with them. The Schulers were kind enough to introduce themselves the day we moved to our house. Tim behaved in a dreadfully aloof manner that day, acting like he was above rural life. Since then, the people on our street approached us with a cautious manner due to Tim's first impression. Without constant interaction, remembering the names of the people I passed on our street was tricky.

Looking at a stack of bills addressed to April and Jerome and the teen magazines belonging to Summer and Holly, I figured out the name of the woman I'd be talking to.

At the sound of footsteps, I put the mail back in the basket. Holly appeared at the other end of the hall. "What should I tell her?"

"To take off her shoes and coat! I'll meet her in the sewing room!"

Holly walked down to the hall.

"Mom doesn't want you to see the kitchen because it is a mess. She and my sister were making lefse. She does want to talk to you, though. Please follow me to the sewing room, Ms. Mulroney."

I took off my boots and followed Holly into a room that resembled a womanly office. There was a long table with various paper scraps and cutting tools. In the corner were two faded plush armchairs.

What I didn't see was a sewing machine.

"Mom doesn't sew. She likes paper crafts," Holly explained, "There's just no such thing as a scrapbooking room."

"So, I see," I replied.

April Schuler came in carrying a tray of flat potato bread, butter, sugar, and a couple of beers. Her curly red hair was tangled on top of her head with a barber clip. She wore a Green Bay Packer sweatshirt over a black turtleneck. A couple of blankets were folded over her arms. Holly quickly went to the door to help her.

"Thanks, honey," April said after her arms were relieved, "why don't you help your sister clean up the kitchen?"

"But, Mom, Summer is going to have me clean the entire thing!"

"If you want to eat the lefse you didn't help make then you are going to clean the kitchen."

Holly sulked out of the sewing room. April motioned me to sit at the table in front of the tray she brought in.

"Katie! How good to see you," she greeted.

Katie? April must have overheard Tim calling me Ketty and assumed that it was what I wished to be referred as such.

"It's Catherine. Ketty is the annoying pet name my husband calls me."

April handed me a blanket.

"I hear you. Sometimes my husband thinks he's funny by calling me different months of the year."

April walked the corner near the window to switch on the space heater. "This room gets so chilly in the winter. I move all this stuff to the kitchen table to work on when it is under twenty degrees outside. However, I am sure what we are going to talk about is something the kids shouldn't hear."

"I am not here to talk about Holly," I said.

"I know. If you were, I would have kept Holly in the room," April laughed, "My daughter is a stubborn girl with strong convictions. She can offend people sometimes. That is why I make her stand in front of her critics and listen to them. Eventually, she will learn humility."

April popped open a bottle of beer and handed it to me.

"I don't know if I should be drinking this given my profession."

"You're over twenty-one, right?" April asked.

I nodded.

"Then you can drink it. It's legal. After what I'm about to tell you, you'll need some alcohol in your system. Fix yourself some lefse too."

The bottle April handed me was an ordinary American lager. Growing up visiting British pubs made me a beer snob who was often avoidant of the major American breweries. Thankfully, the sugar in the lefse counteracted with the beer's rice blandness as I washed it down. In fact, I found the combination to be quite pleasant.

April cleared some papers out of the way and sat at the table across from me.

"I didn't grow up too far from you," she stated, "My family lived in Lindstrom."

"I know where that is," I said, "It's that little Swedish themed town on Highway Eight."

"That's right. I lived there until I went college."

"You went to school at University of North Dakota?" I asked, recalling that Holly mentioned residing in Grand Forks.

"I did. I got my master's in nursing there. Jerome and I both attended the University of Minnesota in Crookston for our undergrads. Jerome studied Manufacturing Management there and agreed to follow me to Grand Forks after we graduated. My uncle's wife helped him get hired up here at John Deer after I graduated from at UND. The plant owner is her brother. Her brother also let us rent the house they grew up in."

"That was very nice of them," I commented. "Were they familiars of your next-door neighbors?"

April twirled her beer bottle around the table. "When Holly came home from school talking about your brother I thought there were some things you needed to know, Catherine, but I didn't know how to approach you. I am very glad you have come over."

I was surprised at April's statement. "Did you know my brother?"

"I didn't know anyone from Stillwater when I was thirteen."

"You knew the Hans, then?"

"I ran into Gladys Han every once in a while. She seemed okay. She was always kind to the girls. She got too old to care for herself. She lives at the Sheyenne Care Center now. My aunt knew her son Cody. When I told my aunt that your brother was the Rhinelander boy, she said she always wished she called the FBI with a tip of who could have done it."

"What could your aunt possibly know?"

"My aunt, Maxine, went to school with Cody Han. She said he was cute, but everyone could tell he just wasn't right in the head. Nobody his age wanted to date him. He started asking twelve-year-old's out when he was a junior in high school."

"Twelve-year-old girls?"

"The way my aunt explained it to me is that gender didn't matter. Folks around here believed that a boy fought back, and Cody no longer attempted to prey on middle schoolers. No one speaks of it beyond rumor given the accusations. I know damn well not to ask questions. Whatever happened, Cody turned to preying on the mentally challenged after that."

"How could he have access to them?" I asked. "They are a protected population."

"He had access to his cousin," April explained, "Gloria Stiejim."

"Stiejim! As in Cheif Stiejim?"

April nodded. "She's his daughter."

I sat dumbfounded. It was easy for me to figure Stiejim was protecting someone when I walked home from the station, but the guy who attacked his daughter? Even if it was his nephew, I couldn't see the logic behind Stiejim projecting all possible blame from Han to my family.

"It was said that Bruce and Linda Stiejim had an unshakable marriage," April said, "No matter the challenges they faced with their daughter's disabilities, they remained stable. One day Linda left. She claimed to the people she was close to that the programs for the disabled in Minnesota were superior to our program here. She claimed that Bruce wasn't in agreement, so she had to get a divorce. A bunch of hokum, I tell you. Being on the board of the Open Door Center, I know what Valley City offers the disable is just as good as any program in Minnesota, if not more so."

"Quite true," I agreed.

"My aunt told me Bruce would follow Gloria and Linda anywhere. If Minnesota truly was the best for Gloria, he would have quit his job. Linda just left and they never spoke since. Then there was the event that happened the weekend after Linda had left that was quite curious."

"What happened?" I asked as April chewed a piece of lefse.

"Cody liked to drive to a slough west of town to drink. Rumor has it that a bunch of men wearing ski masks followed him one night. They stripped Cody and beat him then drove off leaving him for dead. No one was willing to stand around and verify the fact. Somehow Cody made it back to Valley City. He begged Stiejim to investigate. Stiejim wouldn't."

"Because of his daughter?"

"Because he led the pack of men who attacked Cody," April answered. "Now this is something we don't blab about publicly.

Fathers of the children who Cody preyed on approached Stiejim to seek revenge. They feared Stiejim wanted no part given that Cody was his nephew. You see, Gladys and Bruce were part of a large farming family near Lisbon. She was the oldest of thirteen kids, and he was the youngest. She must have been in charge of caring for the younger children and practically raised him. That must be why Bruce asked to be stationed In Valley City and decided to care for her after Cody left."

"I am confused. Are you telling me that Stiejim did seek revenge on his nephew after he molested his daughter?"

"That is common knowledge around here. Rumor has it that Bruce threatened Cody to drop the matter, or he would investigate the accusations against him. Cody packed up and left Valley City altogether. Gladys mentioned to me that he was a traveling salesman one time when we saw each other in the yard..."

"Mom!" we heard Holly yelled, "Summer is drinking a beer!"

"I'm confirmed, you snitch!"

April excused herself, "Just a moment."

April walked out shouting, "Summer Rae Schuler, you put that bottle down!"

Muffled angry voices floated through the walls. I found that a fifteen-year-old having the gall to drink a beer while her parents were awake amusing. Growing up, Tim and I always snuck our liquor in the dorms after midnight. By then the dorm masters were long passed out from their own discreet drinking.

Drinking my beer, I mulled over what April told me, unable to make sense of any of it. Stiejim knew that Cody molested his daughter. His wife left him because his nephew committed the crime. He was willing to kill Cody, yet not ready to arrest him let alone charge him with the crime. The only thing I could be sure of was that Stiejim had some twisted agenda.

Tired of my futile attempt to contemplate Stiejim's illogical motives, I focused my attention on looking through April's crafts scattered around the table. She made cards with each member of the family's picture cut out as an ornament. Another unwelcomed thought popped into my brain.

After Grandma Alice's death, I helped Uncle Oswald and Aunt Rebecca clear out her closet. I looked through the shoe boxes she stored letters and cards she received. One box I came across saved the Christmas cards sent by my parents. Starting the year of Jake's birth my parents took a family photo for the annual Christmas card. Twelve cards showed my mother with her hair combed smiling at her sons. My father stood as a proud man. My brothers gave mischievous grins. Then there was one with my mother smiling a sad smile, holding her infant daughter. My dad stood sternly. Andrew made an awkward attempt to smile. Nick didn't. Joe appeared not to be aware of the camera in front of him. I threw the box in the outside trash can. I never uttered it, but I was always angry at the living members of my family for lacking the ability to fake happiness to celebrate my birth.

April came back in.

"My oldest girl got confused about the alcohol rule," she explained. "Summer was confirmed as a member of our church this past spring. Now she can have a glass of beer or wine at family events. A lot of Christian families around here have that rule. If a teenager makes the mature decision to accept Christ as their savior, then they should receive an adult privilege, within reason of course."

"Of course," I said.

April took another sip of her beer. "Gosh, how are you are doing with all this craziness going on?"

"There are some things I still I don't understand," I answered, "If Stiejim was a cop why didn't he arrest Cody for molesting his daughter if he knew what had happened?"

"Honey, we are talking the early seventies here," April said. "Children and the disable didn't have the creditability they have now. Besides, Stiejim wouldn't have been near this case as a cop considering he was the alleged victim's father. That is why he led the mob to kill Cody."

"Stiejim is trying to blame my family for my brother's death!" I blurted.

"That's not right," April commented, "well, maybe he is trying to be objective, and it just looks like he is putting the blame on you."

In my dealings with Stiejim, I didn't think that could be the case. I smiled at April.

"Thank you so much for your hospitality and taking the time to talk to me."

"Oh, my pleasure," April said as we got up and shook hands. "If you need anything during this time, do not be afraid to come over and ask."

"Thank you."

April walked me to the entryway where my boots were. "How's your mother handling the news?"

My hair fell over my face as I bent over to put my boots on. Thankfully April couldn't see my eyes bulge out of my sockets like a deer in headlights. The last thing I wanted to do was get into my broken family dynamics. At least by the time I rose my head, I formulated an answer.

"Well, the news is quite shocking," I said, "I haven't easily digested it yet. No one seems to believe it..."

"I can only imagine," said April, "and I don't want to."

I opened the door. "Thank you again, April, for everything."

When I heard April close the door behind me, I started to run. Off I went into town again.

9

Somehow, I ran from my street to the Valley City Police Station without slipping on ice on the road or being hit by a car.

Sheriff Nygren was exiting the Barnes County Sherriff side of the building as I approached the door. He looked at me with astonishment at the sight of my chapped cheeks and snot running down my nose. I wiped the snot away with my coat sleeve.

"Mrs. Mulroney, you got people looking for you," Nygren said, "what are you doing here?"

"I am going to tell you who you need to arrest for the murder of my brother!" I shouted, "But first, let discuss the matter of Bruce Stiejim obstructing justice!"

"Obstruction of justice?" Nygreen shook his head, "Let me guess; you were talking to Maxine Anderson's husband's niece. Let me tell you this, Mrs. Mulroney. April Schuler doesn't know the entire story and neither do you."

"I know more than you think!"

Nygren took my arm and led me to his car. "If you feel the need to confront Captain Stiejim, I'll bring you to him."

"Where are you taking me?"

Nygren opened the passenger door to his car. "I am taking you to your house. That is where he is."

"What?"

Nygren drove us to my house without saying a word. I kept quiet figuring at this point, anything I say would implicate me if I spoke. Cops had a way of twisting words.

We pulled up to the driveway. As the sheriff car parked in our driveway I got up and bolted to the door. The first thing I saw was Tim's disapproving face as I enter the kitchen.

"Where have you been?" He barked.

"Why is there a police car in front of our house?"

"Because a dead body was found in our yard that happened to be your brother!" Tim screamed, "And from what I heard, you ran out like a crazy woman at the police station!"

"Don't call me crazy," I said curtly.

Jacob came into the kitchen carrying his luggage. "Okay, Dad, I got my rucksack all packed."

"Rucksack?" I replied, "What does Jacob need a rucksack for?"

Tim pointed towards the door. His luggage and Maggie's diaper bag were waiting in the hallway.

"We are getting kicked out of the house," Tim explained, "Stiejim said that the FBI is coming to search the property. Don't worry; the cops got us set up at the Wagon Wheel Inn."

"We are not getting kicked out of our house!" I screamed.

"Take that up with Stiejim," Tim remarked, "He is downstairs."

I ran downstairs to the basement. Stiejim stood near my washing machine looking at the gray brick wall next to it. He eyed me as I ran down the steps. He stuck out his hand to silence me before I could say anything.

"Ever wonder why there is a gray brick wall in your basement when the other walls are only poured in cement?"

"Ask your sister, Gladys, or her son, Cody," I remarked.

Stiejim grunted. "So you heard about Cody?"

"I have."

"Gladys always did her best to protect him. He was a monster, but he was her son."

Stiejim turned from the wall and stared at me.

"Now, Ms. Mulroney, you have to understand I am between a rock and a hard place. I was never blind to Cody's deeds. I even tried killing him myself," he chuckled then his voice entered in his usual stern tone. "However, we got your son seeing ghosts and your family having a history of mental illness. Now you were aware that your father dealt with substance abuse?"

"I remember."

"Did you know he used to beat your brothers?"

I shook my head, "All I got was verbal abuse the rare time I visited his house. I lived..."

"With your paternal grandmother," Stiejim finished, "You told me. It is also in your brother Joe's file at the State hospital. However, mental illness is hereditary. I am a cop. I must look at all angles. Jacob needs to be tested and I need to knock down this wall. Those are our tasks to reveal the truth."

"Why does my son have to be tested?" I asked, "He didn't kill Jake. It was either my dad or your nephew."

"Things will come out," Stiejim said, "things that could lead us to the right direction. I am not the villain you think I am. I must be tough and fair when it comes to the law."

"Are you telling me you would arrest Cody if he is the man who killed my brother?"

"The FBI will arrest Cody if he is indeed the killer," Stiejim replied. "Now pack your things. You are going to be at the Wagon Wheel Inn for a while."

I turned to walk up the stairs. I felt Stiejim footsteps vibrate from behind. Then he I heard him chuckle.

"Seriously, didn't you wonder why there was a window to the side of your house down here but never any sunshine coming through?"

"I guess I chalked it up to a flaw in the remodeling process," I breathed.

Stiejim let out a snort.

Nygren drove Jacob and me to the Wagon Wheel Inn. Stiejim drove Tim and Maggie. Stiejim volunteered to drive Tim, most likely so they could joke at my expense. Jacob rode with me so Tim could transport his birthday and Christmas presents without the chance of Jacob seeing them. Maggie still experienced toddler oblivion.

"Are we going to jail, Mum?" Jacob asked as Nygren pulled out of our driveway.

"No, Jacob," I answered, "we are just going on a little vacation."

"Why's the cop taking us?" he asked, "Where is he taking us? Are we going to a concentration camp?"

"Where did you heard about those?" I asked, baffled how my first grader could already know about the Holocaust.

"Jake told me about how he learned about Nazis in school."

Seventh grade was when they started teaching about World War II in school, at least in depth. Jake was in seventh grade when he died. I shook my head at the notion that my brother's ghost was haunting my son.

Nygren drove us passed VCSU's campus and up the hill on Winter Show Road. When the car approached the Wagon Wheel Inn, Jacob commented, "Up the hill is not a vacation."

"Yes, it is," I insisted.

"No, it's not. We are in the same town we live in."

"It's a hotel," I snapped, "It will be fun."

Jacob gave me a look to indicate that he was not convinced.

Nygren led Jacob and me to the inn's western style lobby. Tim followed us holding Maggie. Stiejim stepped in from of everyone to approach the front desk. He dinged the tiny service bell signaling a middle-aged woman in a blue polo shirt.

"Hi, Bruce," she greeted.

"Mindy, this is the family I was telling you about," Stiejim explained.

Mindy turned her eyes to us, "The one who rent your sister's house? You poor things."

"We're not poor," Jacob replied, "The cops are just giving us a vacation."

Mindy reached behind the desk and pulled out two miniature candy canes. She handed one to each of my children. "You are in good hands, Little Guy."

Mindy walked out the front desk and handed Stiejim the keys. She motioned the group to follow her. Stiejim and Nygren took our heavy luggage and followed her as Tim and I gather our children's things.

"You caught a stroke of luck, Bruce," Mindy said as we walked down the dim hallway, "The Dunbar family usually reserves this suite during the holidays for their family reunion. This year the family is traveling to Montana for their reunion. Do you remember Missy Dunbar?"

"I gave her a few speeding tickets," Stiejim answered.

"Well, she is now Missy Hunter. She and Justin Hunter married a couple of years ago. They moved to Montana when Justin got that banking job over there. They just had a baby boy, named him Logan."

"I heard," Stiejim replied, "I still go ice fishing with James Hunter on occasion. James said he and Deborah were riding up with Connie and Jim in the Dunbar's Winnebago."

"Ah, it seems like only yesterday that I taught them Sunday school," Mindy replied, "They hated each other. He was always pitching her and she was always kicking him. Look at them now."

Mindy opened a door. Inside were two full beds, a television, bathroom, and a kitchenette. It was nice, but it wasn't home. Then again, my house was becoming more of a graveyard than a home. I questioned if we could find home again.

"Now, if you need anything, please let me know," Mindy said to me as she walked down the hall.

The kids ran into the room. Jacob started bouncing on one of the beds. I had to run in to stop him and Maggie, who was starting to climb the dresser. Tim remained in the doorway talking to Stiejim and Nygren.

"Your son is scheduled to see the psychologist tomorrow morning at ten," Stiejim explained.

"Are you going to be driving us?" Tim asked.

"Why would I be driving you?"

"You wouldn't let us drive our car here," Tim remarked, "Either one of you drive us or drive our car here."

"Come on, Bruce. He's not going to leave town," Nygren said,

"Why don't you drive me to their place to pick up the car? I'll drive it over to them."

"Very well," Stiejim gruffed.

As he followed Nygren out, Stiejim pulled out my smartphone out of his pocket. "You left this at the station."

Tim shut the door before I could thank him. I shook my head at his rudeness while I turned the television on to a kid's station. Jacob and Maggie sat on a bed to watch it. Tim grabbed our suitcases. Instead of unpacking them he started throwing them around. Maggie cried at the commotion.

"Timlin Mulroney, what on earth are you doing?" I shouted as I went to hold Maggie.

"This is great!" Tim ranted, "This is just great! It's bloody Christmas, and we are kicked out of our house because of your crazy family!"

"This isn't my fault," I protested, "Now calm yourself down! You're frightening the children!"

Tim pointed to our son staring at the television. "Jacob's not scared. He is too crazy to be afraid."

"He's not crazy!" I defended, "He's just experienced your rant and raves too many times to be affected by them! If he truly is insane, it's all because you couldn't control your temper! "

Tim opened the door. "I think I saw what resembled a bar in the lobby. I am going there!"

A good wife would have prevented her husband from going to a rumored biker bar. I was livid at Tim. I figured if he got stabbed, he deserved it. Leave it to him to bail on me after we were forced to leave our home.

It was dinnertime. I had nothing to feed my kids. The only food in my possession was a granola bar in my purse. How could I feed my children with only a granola bar?

I walked into the bathroom. I grabbed a hand towel from the towel rack. Sitting on the toilet, I buried my face in the towel and cried out of sheer helplessness. After Grandma Alice had died, I thought I would never feel that way again. I was too naïve at thirteen to realized that things could get worst. Twenty years later here I was with no home, no food, and no support of loved ones.

A knock echoed from the other side of the door. I pushed my face further into my towel to quiet my sobs. Jacob called out, "Mum, Aunt Anna is on the phone. She keeps yelling at me that she wants to speak to an adult."

I wiped my face with the towel. Jacob stood outside the door with Tim's smartphone in his hands. I reached out for it. Anna had a bothersome habit of calling her brother to gush about whatever holiday gala she attended back in England. The sheer purpose of her calls was to belittle the fact our family lived a "lowly life" in Middle America.

"Hello, Anna, it's Catherine. Your brother is not here. He decided to abandon his family at what he would refer to as a "roach motel" to drink himself into oblivion. Don't worry about your poor American relations for a second, Dear Anna. We rather be shacking up in our lowly lot than rubbing elbows with your highbrow friends any year. Merry Christmas."

"Why I ought..." was all I heard as I press the "end call" button on the touch screen. Tim surely would receive an earful from his sister regarding my "ill-mannered behavior". It served him right after he left to get drunk.

There was a knock at the door. Tim had left without his key. I wasn't going to readily let him in after his rant. I called out, "Hello?"

"It's Sherriff Nygren. I have your car keys."

Nygren had more than just the keys to our car. Opening the door, I found him hold two paper bags.

"I hope you don't mind, but I went to pick your family up some burgers and fries."

"Not at all!" I exclaimed, "Come in."

Nygren walked into the room and dropped the bags off at the table. Jacob and Maggie jumped off the bed they were sitting and ran towards the food.

"I was going to pack up some of your crock pots, but Bruce said it would be best just to leave the food for the FBI agents who are going to knock down the basement wall. He believes that they deserve a home cook meal. However, once word gets around that you were ousted from your house more hot dishes will be coming your way. Most likely you will be the recipient of many church youth projects in the area this Christmas. The kids like to cook food."

I wanted to outright hug Nygren for his kindness; however, men in the northern states found the gesture quite awkward. To him, his providing my family food was simply his call of duty to ensure that the people in his town were cared for.

Nygreen tipped his hat to me, "If I don't see you before, Merry Christmas."

"Thank you for the food," Jacob called out as Nygreen exited our room.

I arranged the food for the children on the table and turned on the TV so we could watch Christmas Cartoons during dinner.

At nine o'clock, I had the kids in bed. Maggie slept next to me while Jacob slept in the bed he would share with Tim, who still hadn't returned. Both kids had their eyes closed, yet I could tell neither was asleep. Jacob constantly tossed and turned underneath his sheet. Maggie let out a whimper every thirty seconds. There was nothing much I could do to soothe my restless children because there wasn't a way I could return them to the comfort of their own beds.

I couldn't sleep either. I attempt to distract myself from our situation by reading "A Christmas Carol." My mind kept wandering to my anger towards the entire situation. At one moment I was fuming at Cody Han for taking my brother. Another moment the memory of Stiejim's interrogation fueled my internal wrath. Of course, Tim attributed to my anger, although anger towards him was futile. He became my friend despite his lack of abilities to be emotionally supportive. I married him knowing damn well he was never going to change. All this anger wasted my energy; yet, my rational mind could only help me keep it all inside. At times, I wasn't successful in that. Something had to have come out of my mouth for I heard Jacob utter, "Mum, what are you talking about?"

"Nothing," I replied, "Go to sleep, my dear."

My phone rang. I walked over to my purse. Arizona popped up as the caller's location. "Hello?"

"Catherine? It's Rebecca."

Even though my Uncle Oswald died, Aunt Rebecca still called on our birthdays and Christmas, exactly on the days of and never in the evening.

"Rebecca? Is everything okay?"

"I was hoping you would tell me," Rebecca replied, "I got a voice message from a Bruce Stiejim today. He said his was with the Valley City Police Department. Then I got another message from the FBI! Are you and the kids alright?"

Great, the last thing I wanted to do was to let Rebecca on to what was going on. I didn't know how to explain the situation to myself and have it make sense! If I didn't tell Rebecca what was happening, she'd be on the next flight up north. She still took on the responsibility of my caregiver when she felt I needed one.

I let out a sight. "The police found Jake's body."

"What! Where? How?"

"Jake was buried here in Valley City," I said. "It was a cop's sister's residence where they discovered his body. The kids of the people that rent the place were digging up their yard and found the corpse."

"Oh my god!" Aunt Rebecca exclaimed. "What were the chances? How did they find you?"

Because Jake's ghost led my son to his corpse in my backyard.

I couldn't tell Aunt Rebecca the truth. I never knew how she perceived my family's mental illness. Whatever opinions she had towards my dysfunctional family she kept to herself. I didn't want to risk being lumped into a possible bad opinion with the other Rhinelanders.

"Do you parents know?" Aunt Rebecca asked.

"Well, if the police found me and found you all the way in Arizona, then it's perfectly plausible that they located my parents," I said.

"You haven't tried calling them?"

I didn't know if either of my parents was alive until Aunt Rebecca asked if they knew about Jake's body. Aunt Rebecca was privy to the fact I never maintained contact with my immediate family since I boarded the plane for England. Why she was perplexed that I hadn't called them was beyond me.

"I don't know where they are!"

"Your father is still in Stillwater," Aunt Rebecca said, "As well as your brother Andrew. Your mother lives in Minneapolis."

I waited for Aunt Rebecca to name the institution my mom resided in. She didn't say anything. Nor did she ask me how I was doing with the fact Jake's body was recovered. Without thinking, I filled broke the silence with, "I know where my brother Joe is. He is here in North Dakota at the state mental institution."

"Oh," Rebecca replied, "be sure to tell your father. He's been looking for Joe and Nick for some time."

Call my father? Rebecca knew darn well that I had no contact with my family beyond her. Why did I have to call a father who was searching for my brothers? Didn't Rebecca remember the last thing my dad said to me was "Jake's dead because you were born a girl"?

Maggie cried out in her sleep.

"Is everything okay?" Rebecca asked on the other end.

"That was Maggie," I said, "I have to go."

"Take care," Rebecca said.

"You too," I replied.

I looked over at Maggie. She slept on her side oblivious to the waking world. I turned off the lamp bolted to the wall, turned, and snuggled Maggie against my chest as I closed my eyes.

I still couldn't sleep. Aunt Rebecca's call caused another train of thoughts drove through my mind. Rationally, I knew that my parents had to be notified that the body of their missing son was found. Yet, I wanted to be selfish and keep it to myself. My parents and my brothers witnessed the living Jake Rhinelander. They had memories of a mutual existence that I never got to share with my own brother. They had memories that were never shared with me. All I had of Jake was his death. The gruesome sight of his corpse was my only experience as Jake's sister-not a memory of him teaching me how to ride a bike or having him defend me from bullies. Just the memory of looking at his rotting corpse in my backyard. As heinous as it was, I now held that day as sacred. I didn't want to share it with anyone who shared his life for they didn't share his life with me!

Tim came stumbling into the room. I was thankful the room was dark; therefore, he couldn't see my tears.

10

Ironically, Tim woke up in better shape to drive than me. Maggie didn't sleep like a baby. She rolled, kicked, and once jumped out of the bed, sleepwalking to the toilet. I observed her for five minutes until I realized I should be carrying her back to bed.

The alarm rang at six in the morning. Tim grumbled as he shut it off. Maggie let out a giggle. I rolled over looking at her sweet smiling face. I closed my eyes.

"Get into the shower," I ordered Tim. "Take Jacob in with you."

"Jacob is eight," Tim whined, "He can take a shower himself. Maggie is awake. You take a shower first. You have to dry your hair anyways."

Tim laid down on the bed during the fifteen minutes it took me to shower Maggie and myself. He remained to lie around as Jacob took his shower while I scrambled to get Maggie dressed. He showered and got dressed while I assisted the kids then admonished me for not being ready in time to leave.

"Thank you, Catherine, for getting the kids ready because my lazy drunken self just didn't have the energy to do it!" I mocked as I headed to the bathroom and to dry my hair.

The woman at the front desk handed us doughnuts, coffees, and juice boxes as we exited through the lobby into the pitch black morning sky. I climbed into the car as Tim buckled up Maggie. From the passenger side, I handed the kids their juices boxes and cake doughnuts. Tim entered the car grumbling, "Why do you get to sit in the passenger seat?"

"Since I didn't get to pass out into a peaceful night sleep like you did," I answered.

"How do you know I am not still drunk?" Tim asked, "If I am, do you really want me to drive?"

"You're Irish," I reminded him, "you're more capable when you are drunk than when you are sober. Besides, if you were still drunk you'd be bearable to be around right now."

Tim turned on the car engine. I peered over my shoulder. Jacob and Maggie were asleep in the back seat. I closed my eyes and drifted off.

Eventually, the sun's brightness reflecting against the snow woke me up. I looked to my left to see Tim wearing his sunglasses. I quickly fished through my purse looking for mine. Looking through the windshield, I saw the exit into Carrington pass by. Jacob and Maggie were sleeping.

"Jacob," I quietly called, "Wake up, Honey."

"Why, Mum?"

"We'll be in Fargo in fifteen minutes. If you want to eat, you better do it now."

"I'm not hungry," Jacob complained as he closed his eyes.

I couldn't argue with him. I loved cake doughnuts, but the powder sugar doughnut wrapped on my lap didn't appeal to me. My stomach was full of active nerves. Everything I ate I'd eventually throw up. Why wastes the food?

I leaned against the passenger window. For miles there was nothing but undisturbed snow. The sight had a calming effect. Before I knew it, I fell asleep again.

I am driving towards Fargo on the Minnesota side. I am sitting in the back seat as a blonde man is driving. In a voice that's not my own, I say, "How far is it, Mister?"

"We have a ways," he replied.

"I really need to use the bathroom."

The car pulls over. The man turns to me. He smiles with upturn corner reminding me of the Joker. "Write your name in the snow."

"Catherine!"

Tim whacked me awake. We were the only car parked in front of a brick building in North Fargo. I helped Jacob out of the car while Tim carried Maggie. A tall man with longish sandy hair wearing a thick flannel shirt and ratty jeans waited for us by the front door.

"You must be the Mulroneys," he greeted as he opened the door for us, "I am Doctor Roman Gubler. Why don't you follow me down the hall to the offices?"

Tim and I responded with quiet, cordial greetings. I walked behind Jacob with my hand on his shoulders feeling like I was leading him to be fodder. Tim stared ahead with his sunglasses still on in an attempt to hide his hangover or his irritation of the situation.

Dr. Gubler stopped in front of a gray room filled with toys.

"I'll have you drop off the kids over here," Dr. Gubler said.

I helped Jacob and Maggie out of their coats. Maggie ran over to a pile of square blocks. Jacob sat down next to her. Dr. Gubler motioned me away from the doorway. I followed him into the wood-paneled office across the hall. Tim and I sat on folding chairs in front of cheap wood panel desk. Dr. Gubler sat down on a ratty office chair. He pulled up a laptop from a duffle bag. His fingers started clicking the keys. Tim started raking a miniature sand garden at the corner of the desk. Sitting near a cluster of small cacti left me nothing to play with. Therefore, I sat anxiously waiting for Dr. Gubler to say something, anything.

Dr. Gubler broke the silence by muttering, "fascinating."

Tim dropped the rake, "What?"

"From what I am reading your son is seeing the ghost of his missing uncle whose body shown up underneath your backyard," Dr. Gubler stated, "at least that is what I have to prove."

"What you are here is to prove that my son is crazy," Tim remarked.

Dr. Gubler clicked a key on his computer. "Apparently, Mrs. Mulroney, your family has a history of mental illness as documented in the reports the Valley City police give me; but how about your family, Mr. Mulroney?"

"It's Catherine's messed up family that caused this mess," Tim irately replied, "I don't see what my family has anything to do with it."

"His sister is an alcoholic," I replied curtly. "Actually, I think every member of his entire family is. They just have a lot of money to cover it up. But it may be a cultural thing rather than an illness. He's from

Ireland."

Dr. Gubler raised an eyebrow. "Is the discord between you two just a result of the stressors from the case or is this normal?"

"You're the shrink," Tim remarked, "Shouldn't you be able to figure that out yourself?"

Dr. Gubler shot a sympathetic glance over to me before turning his chair directly at Tim. "Mr. Mulroney, the FBI contracted me to give the investigators an educated assessment on your son's mental state base on meeting with him for a couple of hours out of his life. Now, believe it or not, I am humble enough to admit that is not the best way to get to know someone. Any information you can provide me with about your son would help me and hopefully him. Now, have you observed Jacob in acts of delusional thinking?"

"You mean like imaginary friends?" I questioned.

Dr. Gubler shrugged, "Does he understand the difference between imaginary friends and the friends he has in reality?"

"He never talked about his friend, 'Jake' in the same context of any other person he knows," I answered.

"Catherine permitted the existence of Jake because she believed some mumbo jumbo that 'Jake' was just the projection of Jacob's Americanized self."

I shot Tim a Look. "You were the one who couldn't figure out that Jacob had an imaginary friend."

Dr. Gubler held up a hand. "Enough. Now, I understand moving across the street can be an adjustment to any child. We can only imagine what an adjustment moving across an ocean was for Jacob. It is not unusual for kids to come up with imaginary friends as a coping mechanism. Moving on, when did you two teach Jacob about death?"

Tim and I looked at each other. We never had as so much as a goldfish to gently demonstrate the concept of dying to our children. In regards to ghosts, Tim and I assumed Jacob's paradigm of them were bed sheets floating around the house as depicted in children cartoons.

"I guess the opportunity never arose," I replied.

"How did you explain to him having an uncle he would never get to
meet?" Dr. Gubler asked.

"Jacob hasn't met any of my brothers," I answered, "I don't think he is aware I have any."

Dr. Gubler raised another eyebrow. He proceeded to question me about my family. I constantly answered that I didn't know what went on at my parent's house due to the fact I lived with Grandma Alice. Dr. Gubler asked Tim questions about his family to which he answered that he didn't see the point in dragging his family into my family's mess. Dr. Gubler typed every response. Suddenly, he closed his computer.

"It's quite evident that neither of you have ties to your family of origins," Dr. Gubler said. "That may or may not matter pending on my conversation with Jacob. My session with him will last about two hours. You are welcome to wait in the break room during our session; but given you have a toddler in tow you might want to go somewhere she can run around. I think West Acres is open this morning. It's the only place in Fargo that I know of that can entertain a toddler during the winter."

"What exactly are you going to do with my boy?" Tim asked.

"I am just going to ask him routine questions," Dr. Gubler said. "Before I do, I just need one of you to sign the consent forms that allows me to release the information I obtain to the FBI."

Dr. Gubler slid papers towards our direction. Tim didn't make a move to collect them. Out of obligation, I took a pen from my purse and signed the release papers. Tim immediately walked out of the room with his hands in the air.

"Don't worry, I won't harm Jacob in the two hours I have him," Dr. Gubler said with shaky assurance.

I smiled a small smile and walked out.

Dr. Gubler went into the playroom and sat beside Jacob, who was working on a jigsaw puzzle. Maggie ran over to me. I gathered her and walked her towards the front door. Tim was leaning against the door.

"Did you really have to sign those papers, Ketty?"

"I had no choice," I said.

"There is always a choice," Tim remarked as he pushed the door open.

I helped Maggie into her coat as Tim walked to the car. Surprisingly, he didn't start the engine and drove off anywhere. I walked Maggie to the car. While buckling her in her car seat, I continued, "We would have most likely been charged with interfering with a police investigation if I didn't sign the papers."

Tim turned on the car even though I was only halfway into the passenger side. "So, you decided to sell out your son to avoid jail?"

I rolled my eyes as I buckled up. "Oh, please! You have sold out your family countless of times."

"When?" Tim demanded.

The countless times Tim could be found at a pub during a family crisis surpassed the number of fingers and toes an average person possessed. "Name a time you haven't," I retorted.

Tim pulled out of the parking lot without saying a word.

The moment we walked into the West Acres Mall Tim walked off with Maggie in the direction of the indoor play area. The blue coffee cup logo of Moxie Java greeted me. I walked in and ordered a seasonal peppermint coffee drink.

The coffee shop was empty of patrons. The college-aged barista spent her time playing on her smartphone. One couldn't blame her. It had to suck working during Christmas Eve. I didn't mind. I was too angry at Tim for insinuating that I harmed our son by complying with the police. I may have snapped at the next person who uttered as much as a hello to me.

I didn't marry Tim for his sensitivity. Him allowing me to cry on his shoulder was the last thing I knew to allow myself to expect. I always hoped that he would gain some emotional maturity as he aged. During these past twenty-four hours he reverted into the Tim I loathed in boarding school.

Ironically, I married Tim because I never felt the need to talk truly to someone. It was something I never was accustomed to growing up, therefore, the ability to effectively communicate never became a prerequisite for the men I got involved with. Now, I was alone, wanting someone to talk to with only a preoccupied barista as company. I couldn't unload my woes on a stranger.

Aunt Rebecca's phone call from last night popped into my head. "You haven't tried calling them?"

Minnesotans had a funny way of telling you to do things by admonishing you for not doing them. Of course, if she simply told me to call them and attempted to give me their phone numbers, I wouldn't have taken them. Aunt Rebecca knew darn well that if I was going to talk to my parents, it would be on my own terms. Now, I needed to speak with anyone who could understand the pain of losing the hope that Jake would return even though he or she lost it long ago.

My father house's phone number was 651-555-3322, a phone

number impossible to forget. I tried when I was younger. My fingers tingled at the strangeness of dialing the number I swore I never would nearly two decades ago. I sweated with each callback tone. Finally, a voice I vaguely remembered answered, "Hello?"

My voice shook, "May I speak to Judy or Allen Rhinelander?"

"Who is this?" the voice screeched.

"I beg your pardon?"

"You are calling MY house asking for Judy or Allen?" the voice yelled, "Who are you?"

The voice on the other end was so harsh it took all my courage to stammer out the question, "Do you know of them?"

"I know they don't live here anymore!"

"Sorry to bother you," I said as I hastily clicked the button to end the call.

The barista shifted her eyes away from her texting over to me. I gave her a smile and she went back to her social media feed.

I clicked the phone number search application on my phone. In the last name slot, I typed, "Rhinelander". In the state slot I picked Minnesota from a drop-down menu. My search generated a few results. Only one interested me, A and J Rhinelander, Stillwater.

Clicking on the link instantly dialed my phone. Thankfully, the woman on the other end sounded nicer, "Hello?"

"Hello, Is this Judy Rhinelander?"

"I am not Judy Rhinelander," the voice said.

"Do you know of her?" I asked.

"I do," the voice answered, "but this is not her house."

"If you can give me some information about her that would be great. I am her...." Then I realized that the call was terminated.

I clicked the search engine application to search for mental institutions. There was nothing in Minneapolis or its surrounding suburbs. My phone started ringing. Tim's face popped up as the caller ID.

"Dr. Gubler called," Tim said. "He is done with Jacob."

"Meet me at the door we came in," I said.

In five minutes, Maggie ran over to me. Tim walked past me into Moxie Java. He ordered a coffee while I assisted Maggie into her hat and mittens. We didn't say a word to each other as we drove to Dr. Gubler's office.

Dr. Gubler greeted Maggie as we walked in the building. "Hi, Maggie, do you want to play with your brother."

Maggie let out a gleeful squeal as she ran into the playroom. Tim and I waved at Jacob before Dr. Gubler ushered us into his office. Tim sat next to the sand again. "What's with all the sand and spiked plants?" Tim abruptly asked.

"I'm originally from Nevada," Dr. Gubler answered as he sat down on his chair. "Now, I know you honestly don't care where I grew up. You are here about your son. Well, I am just going to blurt it out. Jacob sees ghosts."

11

"That is bloody ridiculous," Tim replied.

Dr. Gubler seemed taken aback by Tim's statement. I sat frozen in my chair not knowing what to think. Did Doctor Gubler mean that Jacob saw a ghost because of mental illness? Was he going to confirm that Jacob was delusional?

"Most parents would love if I validated what their child claimed to see, Mr. Mulroney," Dr. Gubler said. "This is the first time I can state without a shadow of a doubt that a child indeed sees a ghost. Essentially, I am saying your kid is not crazy."

I breathed a sigh of relief. Tim wasn't taking Dr. Gubler's explanation. "Either you are trying to break our defenses to get us to divulge information for the FBI, or you are plain crazy, doctor."

"You have a problem with my findings, Mr. Mulroney?"

"Yes, I do!" Tim shouted, "Ghosts don't exist!"
"In the past decade they have been findings that ghost exists,"

Dr. Gubler replied. "I am sure you have seen the show, 'Ghost Hunters.'"

"I don't watch the science fiction station it is on," Tim remarked.

"Touché," Dr. Gubler replied, "still there is Allison Dubois, who's real life was a basis for a television show…"

"I think I read that she was a fake," Tim pointed out.

"Since when did you read an article on a medium?" I asked. "The only thing you read when you aren't reading theatrical scripts are futbol scores."

Tim glared at me, "Are you listening to him?"

"Yes," I answered, "He said our son is not crazy. That is what you are saying, Dr. Gubler?"

"Mrs. Mulroney, I am risking my professional reputation by saying your son isn't crazy given his claim; however, I couldn't find a sign of psychosis. Jacob is a bright kid with a strong sense of what is real and what is not. Here, I'll show you."

Dr. Gubler opened a cabinet behind his desk revealing a computer monitor. Dr. Gubler attached a couple of cables from his laptop. Tim and I watch Dr. Gubler log into a couple of servers until we saw a grainy black and white picture of our son with puzzles pieces strewed in front of him. Dr. Gubler clicked a key from his laptop. Jacob came to life.

"Hi, are you this doctor the cops told me I have to talk to?"

Dr. Gubler's voice came through on the monitor. "I am. My name is Roman."

"Roman? Are you from Rome?"

Dr. Gubler came onto the screen. "No. Rome was just one of my mother's favorite places she visited when she and my dad got married. Now, I heard your full name is Jacob Marley. I think that is cool."

"You do?"

"I do. Jacob Marley is a ghost from 'A Christmas Carol'. That's one of my favorite books."

"You want to trade names?" Jacob asked.

"Trade names?"

"Yes. I'll be Roman and will go to Rome. You can be Jacob Marley and get the same dumb book every year for your birthday."

Dr. Gubler chuckled. "So, Jacob, for the next couple of hours we can play some games and talk about things."

"Like what?" Jacob asked.

"Well, I am the person kids like you come and talk to and tell me about things that are on their minds."

"Good, I have a lot of stuff on my mind."

"You do? Tell me."

"One thing, I don't get why Americans never say they are Americans."

"What do you mean?"

"Everyone in my class says they are Norwegian or Swedish because their great-great-grandfather came to America from Norway or Sweden. The thing is nobody in my class has been to Norway and Sweden."

"I've been to Norway."

"Are you going to say your Norwegian?" Jacob taunted.

"For the sake of this argument, I am simply going to say I am from Nevada and leave it at that."

"Where's Nevada?"

"It's a state southwest of North Dakota."

"Were you born there?"

"I was."

"You see, I can say I'm Irish because I was born in Ireland. I can also say I'm English because I lived in England. I am not going to say I am Spanish just because my great-great-great-great-great grandfather came from Spain."

The screen paused then fast forwarded.

"He goes on that rant for ten more minutes" Dr. Gubler explained.

The video started again with the image of Jacob holding an American football. "Seriously, this is not a football! You don't kick it! You all just run with it and jump on each other. My father says…"

Dr. Gubler fast-forwarded the video again. "He ranted about sports for a while as well. Just let me get to a few more minutes past that."

The video played back with Dr. Gubler and Jacob coloring pictures.

"Who are you drawing?" Dr. Gubler asked in the video.
"I am drawing me and my sister, Maggie."

"Cool. You love Maggie?"

"Yeah, that is why I am drawing a picture of her."

"How old is she?"

"One, she's still a baby." Then Jacob began to gush, "She wears cute little clothes and cute little diapers and I just want to hug and kiss her, BUT NO SODOMY!"

"No Sodomy?"

"Just hugs and kisses," Jacob confirmed, "Hugs and kisses aren't sodomy, are they, Dr. Gubler?"

"Nope, it is quite normal to want to hug and kiss babies," Dr. Gubler assured. "But, Jacob, you have me kind of worry. Not too many kids your age know what sodomy is. Do you know what it is?"

"It's when a person puts his pee-pee where it's not supposed to be."

"Where it is not supposed to be?"

"Like in somebody's butt!"

I gripped the armrest on my chair as I saw the eyebrows of the

Dr.Gubler sitting across from me simultaneously rise with the eyebrows of his video likeness. Tim let out an indecipherable mutter.

Dr. Gubler asked onscreen. "Did someone talk to you about sodomy?"

"Jake did."

"Is Jake a friend of yours?"

"He's too weird to be a friend."

"Tell me about him."

"Well at first he was cool," Jacob began, "I was playing hockey at school when the other boys wanted to play football. Jake came and taught me how to shoot the puck far. He would show up at recess and in my yard to play hockey. One day I shot the puck so hard it bounced off the garage, and I thought the puck went right through him!"

"Oh my! Did that scare you?"

"Nah, I thought that was cool."

"You said Jake was weird," Dr. Gubler mentioned. "Why don't you explain?"

"It happened one day when some black truck stopped by in front of my house," Jacob explained, "There was this guy in there, and he wanted to talk to me. Jake told me not to go up to him. This guy kept asking me if I knew some old lady who lived in the house and Jake told me to run inside. He told me that man hurt children, and I wasn't to talk to him. I ran and locked the door."

"Later that night, Jake appeared in my room. He said he needed to talk to me about the guy. I asked him how the man hurt children. He said I didn't want to know, but I told him I did. Then he told me about the sodomy stuff. I got grossed out and told him to go away. He disappeared."

"You see him disappear?"

"Yeah, he gets lighter and lighter until you can't see him anymore."

"Do you find it weird that he disappears?"

"I asked my dad if people disappear and he said no. Then I saw a cartoon about ghosts, and they vanished almost like Jake did. I got scared and screamed. My dad told me ghost didn't exist. I told Jake that ghost didn't exist and he laughed."

"Why'd he laughed?"

"He told me he was a ghost and he did exist. Then I told him that if he didn't go away, I would hurt him. He told me I couldn't hurt him, he's dead."

Jacob took another piece of paper from the pile between him and Dr. Gubler. I watch him scribble shapeless lines. After a few moments watching him drag the crayon across the paper, Dr. Gubler asked, "Have you seen Jake recently?"

"Yeah, he's been really quiet. He tells me not to talk to him when people are around or else, I'll be locked up for being crazy. They do that you know? He told me his mom got locked up for being sad."

Dr. Gubler paused the video. "I understand your mother, Mrs. Mulroney, was institutionalized the majority of your childhood. Is there any way Jacob could have learned that?"

"I never discussed my mother with him," I answered, "he's never asked questions about her."

Dr. Gubler nodded. His eyes went over to Tim. I looked over at my husband expecting one of his signature rants. Tim snorted, "Why are you both looking at me?"

"Have you told Jacob about my family's issues?" I asked.

"No," Tim shouted, "I figure I don't need to if all this keeps going on!"

Dr. Gubler jotted a few notes down on a tablet of paper before he unpaused the video.

The Dr. Gubler in the video asked, "What has Jake been trying to tell you?"

"He tells me that the dead guy we dug up in my yard is what my mother truly wanted for Christmas. I'm not stupid. Nobody wants a dead guy for Christmas."

"If Jake didn't tell you to dig in your yard, would you have done it?"

Jacob vigorously shook his head. "Grownups don't like it when you dig in the yard. My cousin Morton and I wanted to go fishing at the moor near his house. We dug for worms in the garden. Aunt Anna caught us and paddled our butts."

"That sounds harsh."

Jacob shrugged, "Mum says Aunt Anna is a 'B.' You know what a 'B' is? It's a swear word, but I'll whisper it to you..."

Dr. Gubler pushed out his hand as Jacob leaned towards his ear. "I know what it means to call someone a 'B,' Jacob. You shouldn't be whispering it."

Jacob shrank back to his piece of paper. "Sorry."

Dr. Gubler waved his hand. "It's all part of being a kid. I would like to get back to your friend Jake. Did he mention why he thought your mother would want a dead body for Christmas?"

Jacob went back to scribbling. Without looking at Dr. Gubler, he answered, "If Jake said there was a dead body, I definitely wouldn't have gotten my shovel. Jake spent weeks telling me that what my mother really wanted for Christmas was in the ground. The way he was talking, I thought it was going to be pirate treasure."

"Pirate treasure?"

"Like gold and rubies," Jake explained, "I thought there was going to be a big chest full of them. But it was a dead body."

Dr. Gubler clicked a button on his keyboard and the screen went blank. "It became evident that talking about the corpse was unnerving Jacob. I moved the conversation about what he wanted to do for his birthday while he was in Fargo. I thought he was going to say, 'eat at Space Aliens' because all kids like that restaurant; but, he wants to go to the Fry'n Pan. He said that is where he gets to eat worms and dirt."

"It's chocolate pudding with crushed Oreos and gummy worms," I explained.

"Who cares what dessert Jacob wants!" Tim remarked, "Right now, I want to know what this all means. What are you going to tell the police, Dr. Gubler? Are you truly going to tell them that Jacob sees ghosts?"

"I am going to state that I found no signs of psychosis in Jacob," Dr. Gubler said.

"What if they press on for something?" Tim asked.

"I don't understand what you are asking, Mr. Mulroney."

"My kid claimed to see a ghost! I don't think the cops are going to accept your statement of negative psychosis!" Tim shouted.

"The police usually do accept my statements, Mr. Mulroney."

"Well that's bloody arrogant of you," Tim remarked as he bolted from his chair and walked out of Dr. Gubler's office.

I remained in my seat with a case of shell shock. Here a psychologist diagnosed our son as 'not crazy' and Tim goes off ranting at him to retract the statement. Dr. Gubler tapped his pen.

"Mrs. Mulroney, I do need to point out whereas I didn't find any psychosis in Jacob, I did see some signs of a possible narcissistic disorder."

I looked towards the opened door Tim huffed out moments ago. "It's hereditary."

Dr. Gubler gave an awkward smile. "It's nothing that a strict Upper Midwestern upbringing can't straighten out. I am pretty much done here with you unless there is something else you would like to discuss."

I rose from my chair, "Not really, Dr. Gubler, I thank you for your time. I do apologize for having you work on Christmas Eve."

"It's no bother," Dr. Gubler said as he dismissed me with his hand.

I turned towards the door. When I reached the frame, I turned around.

"Actually, Dr. Gubler, I am wondering about something."

"Okay."

"I am just curious about how Jacob reacted when you told him that Jake was my brother's ghost."

"I didn't tell him."

"You didn't tell..."

"That needs to come from you, Mrs. Mulroney," Dr. Gubler interjected.

"Yes," I answered, "of course."

Dr. Gubler walked over and handed me his business card. "Take this in case additional things come up in the matter. Once your husband calms down, I can refer him to research about ghosts. I know of a few court cases where ghostly encounters helped catch criminals."

"That would be up to Tim," I said.

"Of course," he said as I departed the office.

The playroom across the hall was empty. I walked towards the door to find my family all bundled up and ready to get into the car. It was a welcoming sight... or would have been if it weren't for Tim's scowling face.

Jacob got his birthday wish. We ate at the Fry'n Pan where Jacob and Maggie not only got to eat pancakes for lunch, but they got to eat worms and dirt as well. Our waitress told us the Fargo-Moorhead Sertoma Club sponsored at holiday light display at Lindenwood Park. She insisted we should drive through while we were in town. Tim wanted to be back in Valley City right away, yet Jacob reminded him that it was his birthday and we got to do what he wanted. Given that he started his birthday with a psych evaluation, I insisted we allowed Jacob to have what he wanted.

Tim grumbled the entire drive through the park. Being sick of his attitude, I insisted he sat in the back with Maggie while I drove back to Valley City. Despite being against the law, I moved Jacob's booster seat to the passenger side up front. Within minutes of crossing the last exit into Fargo, Tim was asleep.

Usually, the drive in the dark gave nothing to see. It being December, our eyes were treated to an occasional light display from decorated farmhouses. Silent Night played softly over the radio.

"Is your sister asleep?" I asked.

Jacob looked over the back seat. "I think so."

Thus, began the conversation I never thought I'd had with my son.

"Jacob, I need to talk to you about your friend, Jake."

"Jake is not my friend," Jacob remarked.

"Oh, no, of course not," I answered. "Jake was not supposed to be your friend. However, he was supposed to be your uncle."

"My uncle?"

I couldn't look directly at Jacob when I was driving. In my mind's eye, I saw his face contorting in the same twisted expression I saw on Tim whenever I said something he found weird.

"My parents had five children," I explained. "I am the youngest and the only girl. I was supposed to have four brothers, but only knew three."

"How does someone have three brothers when they suppose to have four?" Jacob asked. "How do you have three brothers? The only uncle I know is Uncle Mark."

"As you can guess, I do not have much contact with them."

"What are their names?"

"Andrew, Joe, and Nick," I answered.

"How come they don't give me presents like Uncle Mark?" Jacob asked, "Or crappy books like Aunt Anna? Or even socks like Grandma Bridget?"

"They don't know you," I explained. "Jacob, I haven't talked to any of my brothers since I was thirteen."

"Why?"

I drew in a huge breath. "You see, Jacob, like Maggie I was born in the United States. I was born in Minnesota."

"In Moorhead?" Jacob asked, naming the only Minnesota town he heard of.

"Actually, I was born on the opposite side of the state to Moorhead. The town I was born in, Stillwater, borders Wisconsin like how Moorhead boarders North Dakota. My parents lived there with four sons. One of them was Jake."

Jacob's eyes grew so large I could see them quite clearly in my peripheral vision. "Jake's a ghost. That means he died."

"Before I was born, a man approached my brothers and drove off with Jake in his car. Jake never was seen again. People believed he was dead but no one knew for sure until now."

"Mum? Was that dead guy buried in our yard Jake?"

"Yes, Jacob, it was my brother. And Jake was right, in a way when he told you that his body was what I had wanted for Christmas. After Jake had disappeared, my family broke apart. Most of my brothers left home, and my parents became very....sick. I lived with my Grandma Alice. When I was a bit older than you, Grandma Alice got cancer. I knew she was going to die. I thought if I prayed to God that Jake would come home, everyone in my family would be healthy and happy again."

I didn't know what else to say. I unloaded too heavy of a burden for my son to carry. I rode in silence for some time. Eventually, Jacob uttered, "That man who took him killed him with sodomy."

I whispered, "Something like that."

Jacob looked straight ahead. "Why did it take forever for Jake to come back?"

"He didn't," I answered, "as you said the man who took him killed him and buried in the backyard."

"He did come back, Mum," Jacob insisted, "He's not alive, but he came back. Ghosts are people coming back from the dead."

"True...."

"So why did it take forever for him to come back?"

"I don't know," I answered, "I mean this all this chaos started when I broke down in front of my class and told them about Jake. They all went running to their church youth group and prayed..."

"More people just needed to believe that Jake could come home," Jacob said, "even if he only came back as a ghost."

It never amazed me how kids could simplify life's complexities. My son answered the question that drove me mad for years. I prayed for Jake, God should have brought him back to me. But I was only one person. It took my students' collective prayers to bring him back.

I reached out and squeezed Jacob's hand certain of all the little boys given to moms across the world I had the most special one of all.

12

Christmas Morning not only brought gifts for Maggie, it also brought the arrival of one of her molars. During teething, Maggie preferred one thing for comfort, her Boo-Boo Bunny. Unfortunately, the pink terrycloth rabbit was frozen in our freezer at home. The allotted dose of pain reliever didn't stop Maggie from wailing. I took the car keys and drove over to our house before Tim could storm to the bar.

The cops told me to stay away from the house while the FBI investigated. I was the sister of deceased whose family was under investigation after all. Still, I just had to leave the inn. Christmas Morning left every one of us to remain downtrodden. Tim did the best he could to make our room merry by borrowing the Christmas props from VCSU. He grabbed the wreaths, lights, and a red velveteen bag. Unfortunately, he wasn't able to get a tree. Telling the kids that Santa left his gift bag in our room didn't produce the same magic as finding gifts under a Christmas tree. In fact, Jacob let on that he was starting to let go of the belief of Santa by saying, "I saw you bring the bag in last night, Dad."

A few odd cars were parked on my street when I turned into the driveway. A tan sedan with Minnesota license plates and a purple bumper stickerwith the word "Coexist" spelled with various religious symbols stood in my driveway. As soon as I got out my car, Sheriff Nygren pulled up behind me. My stomach flipped. Cops in Valley City did things by the book. If they told you to stay away once, they'd arrest you despite if you had a valid excuse. Thankfully Nygren caught me instead of Stiejim. I figured I should just get out and face the music. Besides, Nygren was soft heartened enough to have some sympathy for my teething daughter and might just let me in the house.

"I told the Schulers not to bother you," Nygren announced as he got out of his car. "I told them the woman was probably some poor soul who doesn't have any family and looking for anything to connect to for the holidays. It's a common thing, strangers attaching themselves to tragic crimes. Now, don't you worry, I will escort her off the property."

Nygren proceeded to the backyard. I counted to five then followed. He didn't outright dismiss me. This place was still my rental property. I should know who was trespassing in my yard.

A large woman wearing black with purple scarves wrapped around her shoulders knelt next to the hole. Her hand lovingly stroked the tarp that covered the gaping earth. Nygren slowly approached her. He put his hand on his gun holster.

"Excuse me, Ma'am. I need to ask you to step away from the hole."

The woman continued to stroke the tarp. "He was here. He was here all this time."

"Yes, ma'am, and I have to ask you to step away. You are trespassing on private property here."

The woman didn't budge. "I have more right to be at this exact spot than anyone else."

I stopped as I saw Nygren pulling his gun out. A gasp escaped my lips. Not only did it catch Nygren's attention, but it also caused the woman turned away from her vigil. She had a plump face. Her black hair apparently came from a bottle. Her face was a stranger, yet, I oddly recognized it. She looked at the gun Nygren was holding and put her hands up.

"I am just a woman in mourning, Sir. I mean no harm."

"Ma'am, this is an active crime scene. I am going to ask you to leave."

"May I see the house?" the woman asked.

"I cannot permit that," Nygren said, "not without the permission of the owner."

Opportunity presented itself to let me enter the house. "She can if she wants."

"Mrs. Mulroney, you may live here, but you do not own the place," Nygren answered.

"But the owner's son possibly killed my brother, so I was going to work with my lawyer of turning the property owner to my family as a trade fair," I...joked?

If I did joke, Nygren, and the woman were not amused. I turned around embarrassed. I went to the back door, unlocked it, and entered into the house. Standing behind the door, I heard the woman follow me with Nygren's footsteps closely coming behind her. The woman floated through my living room then upstairs. Nygren looked at me befuddled as he quickly chased her.

I raced into the kitchen, quickly grabbing a Ziploc bag from the pantry. There, I found a couple of trial size bags of gourmet coffee. A good cup of coffee potentially could lift Tim and me out of our funk. In my purse, they went. A pink terry cloth face greeted me as I opened the freezer door. Boo-Boo Bunny went into the Ziploc bag before hiding in my purse.

The woman voice filtered down the stairs as I climbed them. "Isn't it procedure to notify the next of kin?"

"The decease's sister just happened to live in our town," Nygren answered. "I am sure you have seen the news, ma'am. This is the case where there is speculation that the deceased haunted his nephew and told him where his body was buried."

Nygren's comment caused me to stop mid-step. Being wrapped up in all of the drama, I didn't have a chance to grab a newspaper or flip on the local network news. I should have figured every news affiliate in the state had reported the story. On average, North Dakota only had seven murders a year in the entire state. If it weren't for local football and the weather, there wouldn't be a need for local news stations. I groaned. No one likes being the talk of the town, even in the caring Midwest.

"Sister?" the woman asked. "The last I heard my daughter got sent off to England…Oh, my!"

I found the woman and Nygren in Maggie's room. Before her birth, I painted it purple and hung pictures of her namesakes. Marguerite's graduation picture from the nineteen seventies hung with Grandma Alice's yearbook photo taken forty years prior. The woman stood underneath Grandma Alice's picture.

"That's Jake's grandmother! What is her picture doing here?"

Nygren looked over at me in the doorway. "Do you know who this woman is, Mrs. Mulroney?"

"Not really."

"Well, she hasn't right out said it; but, from what she has said, she is passing herself off as being the deceased's mother, which I assume would make her your mom."

"That's impossible," I said. "My mother was thin. Her hair color was like this." I tugged on my hair to demonstrate the color. *At least when I saw her twenty years ago*, I thought.

The woman continued to remain fixated on Grandma Alice's portrait. If she were my mother, she would be in her late sixties, early seventies. Ironically, the woman of her elder age standing before me looked younger than the lifeless flesh covered pile of bones laying across the chaise lounge I saw decades ago.

Nygren got impatient with us standing in Maggie's room. "Excuse me, Ms..."

The woman didn't answer readily. Nygren let out a short whistle. She turned around, "Ah, yes. My name is Judy Shipley. Jacob Rhinelander is my son."

Nygren turned to me, "Can you corroborate that Mrs. Mulroney?"

Oh gosh, could I? People changed over the course of two decades. My mother could have dyed her hair and started eating again. My mother's name was Judith. She could have been born Judith Shipley for all I knew. I never met any of my maternal relatives; therefore, never knew my own mother's maiden name. Nygren looked at me for a definite answer. I stood there feeling my organs liquefying.

"Why are you asking her to corroborate my claim?" the woman asked.

"If you have been listening ma'am, you would have heard me referring to this woman is the sister of Jacob Rhinelander," Nygren explained. "If you are who you claimed, then you'd be her mother too."

I stammered, "I really can't say for a fact..."

"Catherine!" the woman exclaimed as she reached out and touched my face. "They told me you are the female version of Jake. At least you were when you were a child."

Suddenly I found myself smothered between her heaving bosom and arms unable to hear nothing but the echo of sobs within her chest. It felt too awkward being in the arms of a stranger, my own mother.

"Ms. Shipley, may I ask how you heard about your son's body being recovered if this is the first time you have met with Mrs. Mulroney?" asked Nygren.

Judy ceased her sob. "I was visiting my son Joe for Christmas. He told me that the cops visited him and asked him questions."

"Your son Joe?"

"Yes," Judy agreed, "He is in Jamestown. That is the town an hour west of here."

"How did he know of the place?" Nygren interrogated.

"He didn't," Judy answered. "I saw the town's water tower when I was heading back to The Cities. I figured I drive around. I saw the police tape around the yard and figured this to be the place."

Judy loosened her embraced and took another look at me and smiled.

"Well, Ms. Shipley, I hope you have intent on staying in Valley City," Nygren said, "The FBI have taken over the case. They'll have questions."

"Oh, sure! Sure, I would," Judy said.

Amid all the commotion, Nygren made arrangements for Judy to stay at the Wagon Wheel Inn and I drove back with a melted Boo-Boo Bunny in my purse.

"Where in the bloody hell have you been?" Tim shouted.

"Getting Boo-Boo Bunny for Maggie," I said exhaustedly.

I grabbed the bag out of my purse and tossed it over to him. It landed on the table next to where he was holding Maggie.

"It's thawed!" he exclaimed.

"Not now, Tim," I groaned as I tossed myself on the bed.

Maggie slurped on Boo-Boo Bunny's wet ears. I closed my eyes with the hope of getting some sleep despite the beeping of Jacob's video game. Right when I felt myself drifting off, someone knocked on our door. Maggie let out a shriek. I open my eyes to catch Tim in mid-curse.

"I'll get it," I said, "just stay with Maggie."

I opened the door to find Judy at the other side. The obvious action of inviting her in didn't enter my sleep deprived mind. I stood in shock stammering, "Judy? What's the matter?"

"Nothing is the matter, my dear," she said meekly. "The lady at the front desk told me where you were. I just thought I'd see my family."

I blushed at the fact I felt violated and resentful towards my mother instead of wanting to graciously let her into my motel room. Still overwhelmed from what transpired this morning, I needed some rest before I got the family ready to go to President Vickerson's house for the Christmas party. My mother had been absence from my life for so long I didn't figure I ought to work in introducing her to my family sometime during the day. Now she stood in front of the door.

"Come on in," I whispered.

Judy walked into the room. Tim shot me a look. Putting my hand on Judy's arm, I announced, "Tim, this is Judy Shipley, my mother."

"Oh," Tim said.

With that, he got up, handed Maggie to me, took his suitcase, and locked himself in the bathroom. Within seconds, we heard the shower start running. Maggie gurgled, turning our focus to her.

"Now who is this sweet baby?" Judy asked.

"Boo-Boo," said Maggie pushing the terry cloth rabbit in front of her.

"That's Maggie," I answered.

Jacob remained on the bed playing his video game.

"Jacob, come met your grandmother."

Jacob continued to play his game.

"Jacob. Jacob. Jacob!"

Jacob threw his handheld onto the mattress. "This level is a bloody pain in the barse!"

"Jacob! Language!"

Jacob looked over at Judy. "Are you American?"

"I am," Judy answered.

"It's all right, Mum," Jacob replied, "Americans don't know what 'barse' is."

"You are not supposed to know what a 'barse' is," I answered.

Judy walked over to the bed. "Hello, Jacob, do you understand who I am?"

Jacob picked up his game. "You're Jake's mum."

Judy's voice started to crack. "Yes, that is right. I heard that you have talked to Jake. Have you seen Jake?"

"I see him right now," Jacob said rather annoyed. "He told me you're his mum."

Judy started crying, "Where is he?"

"Sitting over here," Jacob stated as if it were obvious.

Judy crumpled on the bed bawling. Tim emerged from the bathroom showered and fully dressed. He motioned me to the door. With Maggie in my arms, we walked out into the halls.

"What the hell is all that?" he shouted.

I immediately covered Maggie's ears and mouthed, "Language".

"All right, Catherine, is it true that woman is your mother?"

"Yes."

"The one who was in the loony bin?"

"Well, she is out now."

"For how long?"

"Well, I don't know," I answered, "we haven't gotten to that part yet."

"You haven't gotten to that part, yet!" Tim yelled. "There is a crazy woman crying in our room, and you haven't asked how long she has been sane if she even has been cleared at all?"

"Lower your voice!" I whispered, "Really, don't you think you ought to be a tad less judgmental? None of us have behaved these past couples of days sanely. Put yourself in her position. She just found out this morning where her son's body was discovered. That just reopens wounds."

"Then she needs to learn to deal with it," Tim replied.

"Shall she drink away her sorrows after popping a bunch of pills like your sister, Anna?"

"Sure!" Tim exclaimed, "Because no one wants to be bother with other people's grief. It is called 'social awareness'."

"Like you should be lecturing me about social awareness," I retorted, "You are the biggest solipsist I know."

Tim threw his arms in the air. Then he put his head in his hands. For two minutes I stood watching him alternate gestures while Maggie chomped on Boo-Boo Bunny. Finally, he gained enough composure to ask calmly, "What are we going to do about attending President Vickerson's party?"

"You'll take the kids over there," I answered, "I'll stay behind with her."

"How will I explain your absence?" Tim exclaimed.

"Just say I have relatives coming into town," I explained. "They'll understand. This isn't England. There is no worry about trying to save face. Not when it is fruitless to do so now. The case made the news stations all over the state. We have nothing left to hide from the town."

Tim leaned against me and opened the door behind me. Judy sat on the bed watching Jacob play his video game with red eyes. Tim whistled to motivate Jacob to get dressed. I helped get the kids ready for a Christmas I wouldn't get to spend with them.

I met Judy in the lobby after I showered and dressed. Our plan was to spend the day at the Inn's bar. I found Judy looking inside the bar with a face of apprehension. Peering inside, I saw a bunch of bearded men in leather jackets.

"Yeah, Billy decided to stop by a day early with his crew," Mindy said from behind. "Sorry if you were looking for a quiet place to get a beer."

"Is there any other place to go?" Judy asked.

"It's Christmas Day," I said, "Everything in town is closed."

"Actually, a couple of families celebrate at Sabirs every year," Mindy said. "If they have the dining room open for them, maybe they'll have the lodge open for you. It's only across the street."

Sabir's was Valley City's fine dining establishment. We were guaranteed a good glass of wine if the bar was open. I motioned for Judy to follow me out the door. While we were walking out the door, Holly and Summer Schuler were walking in with a tin foil covered plate.

"Hi, Mrs. Mulroney!" Holly chirped.

Summer gave a lackluster wave.

"Our Uncle Carl announced today that he's a diabetic," Holly announced, "Since you have to eat lefse with sugar, it would be in bad taste to serve it to everyone in front of him. Besides, we have been talking to the cops in your yard..."

"Meaning Holly has been shouting at them from our yard," Summer explained.

"....and they said they really like all the food the town left us. I spoke to Chief Stiejim, and he told me you were kind enough to leave your care packages at your house for the FBI to eat since they don't get to go out as they collect stuff from your house."

"We've seen HAZMAT canisters," Summer added.

"So, we figured you had to leave the lefse we gave you behind," Holly continued reaching the plate outward, "and thought you would like some more."

Accepting the plate from Holly, I said, "Thank you. That was very sweet. Judy, this Holly and Summer Schuler, they live next door to me. Girls, this is my mother, Judy."

"How do you do, Mrs. Rhinelander?" Holly greeted.

"All...right?" Judy answered.

"Well, we got to be going," Holly chirped, "We promised our mom we wouldn't be gone for very long."

"Holly promised," Summer grunted.

"Thank you very much for the lefse, girls. Please give my best to your family."

"We will!" Holly chirped as she walked with a wave.

Judy gave a whooping laugh. "Was that your town's Sandra Dee?"

"Who?" I asked, thickening my English accent so Judy thought me ignorant to her reference.

I lifted the tin foil from the plate. April included a stick of butter and a small tube of white sugar. Judy looked over at the plate.

"What is that?"

"Potato bread you eat with butter and sugar," I answered.

"White bread," Judy snorted, "Your town is what they eat."

Having seen many a Christmas television special as a child, I knew one shouldn't be curt with one's mother during the holidays. Judy's response to Holly and her family's generous offering irked me. I'd seen it before. For community art events, Tim invited artists and musicians from "the cities" as the Twin Cities of Minneapolis and Saint Paul and their surrounding suburbs were referred as in North Dakota. Anyone from that area looked down upon North Dakota as if we were a bunch of ignorant hicks. I expected that behavior from an arrogant young artist, but not from my mother. If she were going to behave as such, the afternoon would be unbearable.

Mindy came up from behind me. "Would you like me to take that back to your room, Mrs. Mulroney?"

"Yes," I answered handing her the tray, "If you would be so kind."

Judy gave me a quizzical look as I turned to the door. "Are you just going to let her go into your room?"

"Mindy? Yes. She has the keys to all the rooms. She's the manager."

"How well do you know her?"

"Well, I only met her two days ago, but she and the rest of the staff have been so kind to my family and me."

"What if she is working for the cops?" Judy asked.

Even though I understood Judy's paranoia, I couldn't help by being a bit annoyed with it. "If she searches my room, I'll report her to her supervisor."

Judy and I walked across the street, silently to Sabir's. Thankfully, they were open. I could have my glass of wine. The waiter told us they didn't have a full kitchen staff that day, but would be able to serve us any appetizers we wanted.

Judy wasn't impressed with the menu. "There is a lot of fried stuff on the menu. It doesn't appear to be very healthy."

"There are other things," I pointed out.

"Strawberry White Zinfandel? Now, that is not real wine."

"Actually, that sounds good," I said, "I'll think I'll have a glass."

"Really? It tastes like Kool-Aid."

Something told me that I needed to drink something that would go down easy. I ordered the Strawberry White Zinfandel and Calamari. Judy ordered a glass of Merlot. The waiter brought out our drinks within seconds.

So, there I was, sitting across to my mother who spent my childhood in insane asylums and didn't think highly of my town. What was there to talk about? I certainly couldn't ask her when she was declared as sane. That would be rude. Yet, I couldn't think of a shared experience between us. My dead brother did not make for pleasant conversation on Christmas. Besides, the woman sitting with me was a stranger despite the fact she once housed me in her uterus. I didn't feel like bearing my soul to her, which I didn't care to do in front of the few people close to me.

"How old is Jake?" Judy asked.

I turned my eyes from the window I didn't realize I as staring out. "Well, the state forensic department determined that Jake died shortly after he was kidnapped."

"I was asking about your son."

"Oh," I answered, "He's Jacob, not Jake. He turned eight on Christmas Eve. His full name is Jacob Marley Mulroney, after the ghost in 'A Christmas Carol'."

"Ahh, he's a little Christmas babe," Judy gushed. "You know, I just love that book. In fact, I nearly named Jake, Jacob Marley. I couldn't though, because of the Rhinelander tradition."

"Rhinelander tradition?"

"Where the sons have their father's first name as their middle name," Judy answered, "all of your brothers' middle names are Allen. Your dad and Uncle Oswald had the middle name, Walter, after your Grandpa Rhinelander."

"I just thought it was something you and Allen did," I replied, "after all, I am Catherine Judith."

Judy beamed. "Now Maggie, what is her full name?"

"Marguerite Alice," I answered. "She named after Tim's stepmother and of course, Grandma Rhinelander."

Judy's smile quickly turned into a grimace.

"Tim is short for Timlin, not Timothy," I rambled. "His full name is Timlin Ryan Mulroney. He's from Ireland."

"I could tell," Judy answered forcing the ire to fade from her voice, "He has an interesting way of speaking."

Good. The conversation hadn't turned completely awkward. Words continued to fall from my mouth. "Jacob was also born in Ireland. I was pregnant with Maggie when Tim got the job at Valley City State University. She will turn two on June 30th …"

The waiter came with our calamari. I shut up to thank him. Now Judy had a window to say anything.

"Jacob has an aunt around his age."

"You have another daughter?"

"No," answered Judy, "Your father does. He got remarried to his girlfriend, Julia. She is about fifteen years younger than him. Their daughter is adorable. Her name is Kylie."

Poor Child, I thought.

"It would have been nice to know I had a grandson to look forward to around that time. I mean, I was expecting the divorce. I knew it was inevitable when I started to get well. Your father and I were very estranged. He didn't think it was right to divorce me when I was committed. He wanted to wait to ensure that I could take care of my own."

I shifted in my seat as Judy declared her entitlement to know my son and referred to my father as a caring person. She continued to speak oblivious to my discomfort.

"Andrew married Kyrsten. I don't know if you remember her. She says she remembers you. Anyways, they have two boys, Keagan and Tristan. Joe has a daughter. Her name is Sadie. She is nine months. Nick was married and divorced. He left the military and lives somewhere in California. His ex-wife, Jesse, still communicates with me. I get to see their daughter, Camille, through Skype once a week."

"Very cool," I absentmindedly responded.

"So, you have been in North Dakota for two years now?" Judy asked.

"It will be in January," I said, taking a sip of wine.

"And you didn't think of contacting anyone?"

"Aunt Rebecca knew," I said. "She was the only one who kept

in touch with me when I was in England."

"Your Aunt Rebecca," Judy said, with hurt in her voice.

"Well," I said, "She took care of me after Grandma Alice died. I didn't think you remembered you had a daughter."

"You thought I forgot I had a daughter?"

Tears edged my eyes. I sucked my breath in hoping that one wouldn't drop. "It's just that I don't have a memory of living in the house with you and Allen. I remember Grandma Alice taking me to visit you a couple of times. You just sat there staring off into space. Then there was that god-awful Christmas your hospital closed."

"Are you talking about Saint Francis?"

"I think that was it," I answered. "It was the Christmas Jake was going to come home. Grandma Alice, Uncle Oswald, and Aunt Rebecca took me to the house. You were laying on the chaise lounge unaware I was there. Allen was drunk and went off on Uncle Oswald. He mentioned Jake was dead, and I shouted that he was wrong. Then he told me that Jake was dead because I was born a girl."

"Oh, honey," Judy sighed.

Then the tear dropped. Quickly I wiped it away. Thickening my accent to shield myself, I explained, "After that, I didn't see a reason to call after I left England. It was made very clear to me that I had no place in the family. I didn't know Jake; therefore, I didn't have a place."

Judy grabbed my hands. "Catherine, you weren't supposed to feel that way."

"I did."

Judy sighed, "It's just we thought you as blessed for not having the experience of losing Jake. At least, your brothers and I did. We thought keeping you away from the pain would give you a chance for a normal life."

"I have the pain of losing Jake. I was born with it. The worst part is I don't have any happy memories of the living Jake to comfort me."

"Sometimes, Catherine, those just make the pain greater."

Suddenly my English propriety broke and my voice rose. "I want to know Jake! I want to know what happened! I just want to know!"

Judy pulled a fifty-dollar bill from her purse and placed it on the table. She walked over, grabbed my hand, and pulled me up from my seat. "We ought to get back to the inn. You ought to know what happened."

13

Judy laid me out on my bed. She started to stroke my hair. Thus, she began the story of the day that trapped her during the last thirty some years.

"It was five days before Christmas. The boys and I spent the afternoon making cookies. Towards early evening, your brothers were so hyped up on sugar that I told them to go outside. The temperature had been in the single digits the week before. It was twenty degrees that day. I needed to make dinner before your father came home. You know he was a court reporter for Washington County, right?"

Frankly, I didn't remember my father having a job. I shook my head.

Judy continued, "Well, he was a court reporter. It was very lucrative but very stressful. It allowed me to stay home with four kids and get by. I tried to make things comfortable as possible for him. Dinner had to be on the table at six. That night I knew I wouldn't have dinner on time with four boys running around the house. I sent them outside.

"There was a small nagging feeling I felt that it might have been against my better judgment to allow the boys to play outside that day. I chocked it up being afraid that the police would end up at my door again. Your brothers got into so much trouble the way boys do. We lived on the corner of Fifth Street North and Myrtle Ave. The year before, the boys had gotten the idea of sledding on the sidewalks of Myrtle to see who could make it the closest to Wisconsin. They never made it to the Saint Croix River. Instead, Joe knocked over a downtown shopper on Main Street. It wasn't until a cop car almost hit Nick did the boys stopped their shenanigans. Your brothers ran back home leaving Nick to deal with the police. Of course, Nick ratted your other brothers out, and the cop ripped them all a new one when he dropped Nick off at home.

"That night, the boys came home themselves, without Jake. All three of them were smiling. I kept asking your brothers where Jake was. One of them would try to say something but got hushed by the others.

"Your father came home that night, and dinner was on the table, still no Jake. I outright demanded that someone tell me where Jake was, or I wasn't serving dinner. Joe yelled out, 'Jake is getting a hundred dollars so we can buy you a really good gift this year, Mom.'

"Then out came the story of how the boys were near the river and a man with the fancy car saw them as he was driving on Main Street. He said he had a job for one of them but only one. He would give a hundred dollars for whoever worked for him. The man asked for the boys' ages. He picked Jake. Jake got in the car, and that is the last any of us saw him.

"I figured out that Jake had been kidnapped and called the cops right away. They came to the house and questioned the boys. Most of the questions involved how the kids were so stupid to let their brother get into the car. One cop even went as far as announcing Jake's death immediately to your brothers. That night when they went to bed, I heard hear them crying that they only wanted to give me a nice present.

"At first, your Grandma Rhinelander was supportive. By that, I mean that she used her daddy's money to buy all the resources she could. Your Uncle Oswald used his influences as a lawyer in the area to work with the people he knew in law enforcement. The whole town rallied around us. Flyers were posted all around Main Street and Myrtle Ave. The local stations ran updates every night. Unfortunately, it wasn't enough. What we needed were clues to finding Jake, which we didn't have. The only witnesses to the kidnapping were your brothers, and they couldn't provide much beyond the man was blonde and the car was fancy and black.

"Jake was kidnapped before Adam Walsh was-you know, the kid of the host of 'America's Most Wanted.' The police didn't have a procedure for obtaining abducted children. The National Center for Missing and Exploited Children didn't exist. Also, I wasn't Patty Wetterling. I just didn't have the strength..."

Patty Wetterling became a known child safety advocate in Minnesota after her son's 1989 kidnapping. I didn't know what I could say to say, how we could even compare to....

Judy continued, "I have major depression. My brother Nicholas and I inherited it from our father."

"You have a brother named Nick?"

"Had a brother named Nick," Judy corrected. "He committed suicide while I was pregnant with Nick."

"Where were your parents during Jake's disappearance?"

"They were killed in a car accident the week I had Joe. Didn't you know?"

I shook my head.

"They were your Grandpa Andy and Grandma Josephine. I was supposed to be naming Joe 'Walter' after your Grandpa Rhinelander. Your Grandma had a conniption that I named him Joseph after my mother. I had already name Andrew after my father. I told her that your dad already gave my sons their middle and last names, I was picking out their first names."

Judy chuckled. I was confused. "That doesn't sound like Grandma Alice."

"She might have changed her tune a bit when you were born," Judy remarked, "She didn't like me much. She didn't think it was fair that your father had to take care of me during my depressive episodes. At the beginning of our marriage, your father and I had a good handle of my depression. I had cases of the baby blues with Jake and Andrew. My parents being killed on their way to see Joe threw me for a loop. I think it was at the insistence of your Grandma Rhinelander that your father had me committed. I went in and it ended up being good for me. When the depression came from losing my brother then giving birth to his namesake shortly after, I voluntarily committed myself for two weeks.

"Somehow, an investigated reporter got wind that I had been institutionalized. In the seventies, seeking voluntary hospitalization was not seen as proactively taking care of yourself. It still isn't, that's why many people ended up harming themselves or others because of the stigma of admitting they have a mental illness. Anyways, the town got suspicious. Rumors started circulating that I had killed Jake and had your brothers made up the story of the man with the fancy car. Public support began to wane. Your father and I were left trying to find Jake with no resources to help us."

Judy's voice broke into a massive empty silence. I expected her to tell me that they roam the world looking for Jake. When Judy didn't speak, I realized the awful truth. "You quit looking."

"Ah, Catherine," Judy sighed, "we never truly gave up. The thing is we needed to know what direction to go in and that we never got. Everyone, they let us grieve for a little while. Then people just expected us to jump back and tend to our responsibilities. The bill collectors demanded to be paid. Teachers would call us and be all like, 'I know your son is missing, but that is no excuse for your other son to not mind his P's and Q's.' People would drop by for random reasons and be appalled that I couldn't keep a sparkling house. Your father and I knew that we had to maintain our normal responsibilities to gain public sympathies, but nothing was normal anymore. The more I tried to fake normalcy, the more I broke.

"Somehow despite our grief, our father and I connected one night. When I discovered I was pregnant we thought it was Jake coming back to us. Everyone rallied around us again expecting a resurrection. Then you were born a girl..."

Judy bawled, drenching the right side of my face with her tears. I reached onto the nightstand to grab the box of tissues. Judy first blew her nose loudly. Suddenly I felt the soft paper wipe of the tissues across my face. Judy chuckled a little. "Sorry."

"No problem," I replied.

"I always wanted a daughter. I had three other boys in hopes I would have a girl. Yet, it was all wrong. You were the sister Jake always wanted. His friend, Alex Hagen, had a brother and a sister. Jake took a shining to Alex's sister Amanda. He wanted a sister just like her. Finally, you were here and he wasn't."

Judy's voice broke again yet, this time, she quickly regained herself. "It was hard. I had a new baby. I also had a son to find and nowhere to look. I had to deal with Andrew seeking comfort with several girls, Joe taking drugs, and Nick's new found affinity for guns which a couple of times he was caught turning one on himself. Your father continued to distance himself by drinking. It was too much for me. I felt myself disconnecting. Strangely, it felt comfortable. All I wanted was peace from the chaos, Catherine. So, I allowed myself to mentally check out. I did so with the belief that I could reenter the world when I was ready. I was mistaken."

I let out an unintended yawn. The details of my family's tragedy drained me. It was time to turn the story. "How were you able to get better?"

"For over twenty years my therapists alternated between electric shock therapy and strong medication. The shock was so I can feel emotions. The medication was to numb them. After Saint Francis had closed, your Uncle Oswald found me a more serene place to recover. There I was assigned a therapist who made the connection that one 'therapy' was only treating the other. In order to get to the root of the problem, I had daily two-hour sessions with her following by a three-hour long session of Dialectic Behavior Therapy. In the DBT sessions, I learned skills to help me cope with the repressed emotions my individual therapist helped me drudge up. Being the saddest case any therapists had ever seen, it took me years to complete such intensive therapy," Judy chuckled, "eventually, they let me out and found me a place to live."

The laughter didn't last long. "My release was bittersweet. I came home recovered, but discovered my family was digging themselves out of ruins. Your father had just started dating Julia. I couldn't begrudge her. She was the woman who helped your dad deal with his alcoholism. Andrew juggled with raising two boys and an immature wife while being the sole breadwinner on a small income. Nick was dealing with troubles in the military because he went AWOL. Your father didn't want to tell me that Joe got incarcerated. It's been a hard decade for all of us, but we have been slowly and surely getting back on our feet.

"I often wondered about you. Half of my recent therapy sessions dealt with how I feel cheated not having a relationship with you. When your father told me that his mother sent you to boarding school, I just wanted to rip his head off. I demanded that he tell me where you were. He said that you told him in no uncertain terms that he was ever to contact him among other things. He said you made it very clear you wished never to associate with him at your grandmother's funeral."

I didn't remember talking to my father at Grandma Alice's funeral. It sounded to me that drunken louse was covering his ass. "He was probably drunk."

"Now, Catherine, he's not a drunk anymore. He went to Hazelden and got help. He has been sober for ten years."

Hazelden was a nationally accredited addiction rehabilitation clinic located in Center City, Minnesota, not too far from Stillwater. Celebrities have been known to go there if they were indeed serious about getting better. Yet, a prestigious rehab center wasn't going to change my image of Allen Rhinelander. No one under any influence should tell their child that they killed their sibling by being born the opposite gender.

Judy started to open her mouth with most likely more words in defense of Allen. Thankfully, Jacob burst through the door.

"Mummy! President Vickerson gave out Christmas poppers just like they do in England! She said I could take some of them back to give to you and Grandma Judy!"

I lift myself from my mother's lap within seconds of Jacob pounce upon it. He pulled a red foiled popper from his coat. "Do you know what a Christmas popper is, Grandma Judy?"

My mother held her grandson on her lap and shook her head. "No. I have never seen one before."

"All you do is pull these ends and..."

"Jacob!" I shouted, "Don't pull the popper near your grandmother's face. Stand away on the floor."

Jacob bounced on the floor and pulled the popper's ends. Suddenly it rained confetti and chocolates. Jacob picked up a piece of candy and handed it over to his grandmother.

"Here, Grandma Judy, you can have this one."

Judy opened her arms with a tear down her face. Jacob jumped into them. Tim burst in holding Maggie. "Catherine, I have decided become a citizen and register as a Democrat!"

I stifled a groan. After years of Tim telling me to keep my mouth shut about the political climates of England and Ireland, I felt anything but enthusiasm for Tim's budding patriotism. "How did you reach the conclusion?"

"I was talking with the professors and as always our conversations turned in the regards to the local and federal political climate. During the discussion, President Vickerson said, 'Timlin, it is such a shame you are not a citizen. You have such fanciful ideas...'"

I interrupted, "President Vickerson commented on you 'fanciful' ideas?"

"More or less," Tim explained.

"Well, that is good," my mother commented, "This state will need more people like you."

With my mom's encouragement, Tim continued his banal litany of how his becoming a democratic citizen would change the world. As always he went on and on, not really caring if Mother and I were listening or pretending to be. The children played with their new toys. Suddenly it was back to the Mulroney normal.

I looked over a Judy smiling and nodding. She was meant to be there with us. She was my mother. She was my family.

14

Red bumps gathered on my face throughout the week. Finally, the white puss poked their tiny heads ready to explode! Yes, it was weird of me to love getting white heads. Somehow, popping them on my face relieved the stress that caused them. I spent fifteen minutes the morning after Christmas popping my face until Tim started yelling at me to get out of the bathroom.

Maggie played with her latest beeping, bopping gadget in between the beds. Jacob sat at the table.

"Morning, Dearie," I said, kissing my son on his head, "what are you up to?"

"Writing a letter to Grandma Bridget," he answered.

I took a glance at the words on the motel's letterhead.

Dear Grandma Bridget,
My dad told me I have to write you a thank you note to thank you for your Christmas gift. Thank you for the socks. Dad says to tell you I appreciate them. I appreciate
them.
I met a new grandma yesterday. Her name is Grandma Judy. She will be my favorite grandma now. She is taking Maggie and me to Pamida to buy whatever we want.

"Jacob Marley!" I screamed, "That is not an appropriate thing to write to your grandmother, even if it is true!"

"You always told me to tell the truth, Mum!"

Tim chuckled, "That's right, my boy! Seriously, my mum ought to know that children never appreciate socks."

Tim pulled on his coat out and grabbed his courier bag. He
saluted me and walked out the door to head for his office. I shook
my head. His tension of being cooped up with the children and me hung
heavy in the air. Intellectuals needed solitudes. Tim became a beast
whenever he went a couple of days without it; therefore, I didn't mind
his hasty retreat.

I dressed the children in the winter gear. Before going to her
room the night before, Judy suggested that she take the kids to Pamida
to pick out their Christmas presents from her then take them out for
pizza. The kids were very excited. They had never had an outing with a
grandparent. Tim's parents only visited Jacob when they were passing
through London, and neither of them made any plans to come to the
States to meet Maggie. In my mother, Jake finally had the grandparent
he could brag about their friends at school.

"Do you think Grandma Judy would take us to Pizza Corner
rather than Pizza Hut?" Jacob asked as we walked down the hall to my
mother's room.

"You can ask," I answered. "Just make sure you are polite about
it. Also, Jacob, I want you to understand that Grandma Judy is the exact
opposite of Grandma Bridget. She will be very generous, but she does
not have the means to be as such. Keep your demands reasonable."

"I know!" Jacob answered as we got to my mother's door.

Jacob knocked. Judy opened it while talking on her cell phone.
She motioned us in. I stood in her room with the kids as she paced the
room uttering, "uh-huh" and "sure, I understand."

"...Seriously, Allen, when your parents bought that burial plot it
was for you to be buried with your wife. You have a wife...Besides, I was
thinking of maybe having a green funeral for Jake. His body wasn't
preserved in chemicals...Well, we can contract the state's Department
of mortuary science."

Judy continued with another round of "umms" and "uh-huh".
Maggie started sweating in her coat causing her to fuss.

"Allen! I got to go!" Judy shouted. "Maggie's here, and she is
getting fussy...Catherine's daughter... Yes, she has a son too; named
Jacob...Catherine is done with school. She moved to North Dakota...I
don't know when, asked her yourself."

Mother motioned the phone towards me. I quickly waved it
away. Judy put it back on her ear, "She's got things to do. I am sure you
will be seeing her soon enough."

Judy finished her called then started profusely apologizing.

"...Your father always has to have everything planned. That's how he copes with stressful situations now that he doesn't drink; he plans everything that is in his control. The only time I ever get a call from him is when we need to deal with one of your brothers..."

Judy kept rambling about dealing with Joe's incarceration and Nick's mental health issues then went on how Allen contacted her in a businesslike manner to address the matters. "...and now that Jake's body has been discovered your father wants to have the burial planned immediately. It was hard to get him off the phone..."

"Who's Mum's father?" Jacob asked.

"Your Grandpa Allen," Judy answered as she knelt down to Jacob's eye level. "You'll get to meet him when we bury your Uncle Jake."

The prospect of seeing my father disgusted me. Trying not to choke on the words I asked, "Allen isn't really coming up to Valley City, is he?"

"No," my mother answered, "Surprisingly, he trusts me in overseeing bringing Jake's body into Stillwater."

Stillwater? Stillwater! I knew darn well I ought not to throw a fit in front of my children against the rationale that my brother was going to be buried in Stillwater-or somewhere within the Twin Cities Metro area. It made sense to buried Jake in the area he grew up than in the town he was killed in, but I lived in that city. I needed to have a sacred place to visit him, and it certainly wasn't going to be near that drunken louse of a father...

"Catherine, are you all right?" Judy asked. "You seem to be somewhere else."

"I'm fine," I said. "I just don't think Tim, or I would be able to get time off of work to attend a burial in Stillwater."

"I think the school district would understand," Judy kindly lectured, "you have to attend your own brother's funeral."

Ugh! Trapped by sentimentality and family obligation, there was no way out of enduring a visit to Stillwater. "I see that the kids are getting antsy. Did Tim leave you Maggie's car seat?"

"Tim left me the car," Judy said. "He said he was going to walk to the University since it was a beautiful day out."

I checked the weather app on my smartphone. The day's high was thirty-three degrees, warmer than average for late December in North Dakota. It would have made a comfortable walk if one dressed properly.

"What are you doing this afternoon, dear?" Mother asked.

"I ought to start writing thank you cards for those who brought us food," I said as I kissed the children.

Judy opened the door, "I suppose that would be a good thing to do while the kids are not underfoot."

I nodded, "Okay, kids, be safe and behave for your grandmother."

"I'm sure they are going to be little angels," Judy cooed as she walked them out the door.

I didn't intend to write thank you cards. My stationary sat in the junk door in my kitchen. Of course, making digital cards was a possibility, a tacky possibility. My eye caught sight of Judy's car keys on her table. I grabbed them then went to my room for my coat. Many holiday visitors vacated the inn by late morning. The staff hastily cleaned rooms. Nobody paid any heed to me as I walked past in the hallway. Nobody asked questions I didn't feel like answering. If they did, I wouldn't have had one. I wasn't sure of my sudden intentions of driving to my house. There was nothing at my house but answers I didn't want to know. During the drive, I silently rationalized, "I need my stationary."

North Dakota's state police parked the medical examination's vehicle in my driveway with the back doors opened. Two officers pushed another gurney across my yard. The small black body bag strapped nearly fell over at the force it took to steer the small wheels through a half of foot of snow. I got out of the car and followed the gurney tracks out back. Stiejim passed me with an inaudible grunt.

"Hello, Captain," I greeted.

Stiejim kept walking. I continued to follow the tracks to the backyard until I saw Nygren in the middle of the yard. The tracks continue to make a path near the storage shed out back, where another grave had been dug out.

"You really don't want to be here right now, Mrs. Mulroney," Nygren sighed. "It's a morbid sight out here."

"They found another child," I replied.

"The FBI agents are looking for two more bodies."

"How are they sure there are two more bodies?" I asked.

"With the case involving a child, the FBI decided to work over

Christmas. Over the past two days, the agents knocked down the brick wall down. Not only did they find evidence that Han sodomized your brother, but they also found evidence of three other children who disappeared during the seventies and eighties. There was Lindsay Briar from Aberdeen, South Dakota, Nadine Tucker from Billings, Montana, and Robbie Hunt from Brandon..."

Nygren's attention was distracted from a crew of agents over by the shed that was padlocked when my family moved. One motioned another into the shed. Nygren shook his head, "Looks like they found another body. Three down..."

"If they are just pulling up bodies, how do they know who the children are?" I asked.

"Han documented his attacks with photographs. The FBI submitted them into a facial recognition database. The portable x-ray machines arrived this morning to locate what is buried in the ground. Thankfully, the graves weren't deep. The body that was just dug up was one of the girls based on the sizes of the pelvis. The body buried in the shed is either the other girl or of Robbie..."

"From Brandon, Minnesota?" I asked.

"From Brandon, Manitoba," Nygren said. "We had to contact the Canadian Bureau to identify him when the FBI search came up with no results, made sense to do so since Manitoba is the Providence north of here. From the date of the photo, it looks like Robbie was the last victim Han brought to the house. If he continued to have a reason to visit Valley City, Han probably abducted a child from Saskatchewan. He seemed to have a pattern of abducting from boarding states and providences going for him."

"What did you mean by saying 'if he had a reason to visit Valley City'?"

Nygren took my elbow and walked me towards the front yard.

"I'd hate to be Bruce Stiejim right now," he began. "He had no choice but to go to his sister and explained the past week's events to her. During that time, she admitted to him that around nineteen eighty-five or eighty-six, Han all but confessed that he molested Gloria. Hearing that, Gladys banished him from the house. Both Gladys and Bruce are working with the FBI in locating Han. Han still sent his mother cards occasionally. His last known whereabouts were in Boulder, Colorado."

"Gladys Han didn't tell Stiejim earlier that her son attacked Gloria?" I asked as we got to the front corner of the house.

Nygren let go of my elbow. "Han was a monster but still her son.

Gladys knew the moment she told Bruce about Gloria he would have killed Han. If that had happened, she would have lost both her brother and her son. In her mind, she was keeping Bruce out of trouble."

"Oh, I see," I replied, "Now you mentioned there were pictures? How were they developed? Wouldn't some photo developer notify the authorities if they saw pictures depicting harm against children?"

"Han used Polaroid film," Nygren answered, "and wrote the dates of the attacks on the boarder below. Even if he used standard film, there wouldn't be a guarantee someone would have to call the police on him. These sick people...well; I know they are more common that you would like to think. Now that I've answered your questions, Ms. Mulroney, may I ask what brought you to the crime scene today?"

"Oh, nothing really," I stammered, "I just need to get my stationary. I have a lot of thank you cards to write. The town's been so kind feeding my family during this ordeal."

Nygren pointed the direction of Central Avenue. "May I suggest you go into one of the town's gift shops and buy yourself a new set? I bought my sister a nice set of locally made greeting cards at The Eagle Nest bookstore." Before I could say anything, he tipped his hat, "Seriously, Ms. Mulroney, you don't want to be near the house."

Nygren walked to the back yard. I walked to my car, but I stood there staring at my reflection in the car window. It was real. Han killed my brother. He killed other children as well. Knowing should have been more than enough for me. It wasn't.

I entered the house through the front. My entryway was cluttered with evidence boxes. Peering into the kitchen, I saw remnants of hot dishes and soda cans strewed all over the counters. Our coffee maker was out with the pot half full.

I took a glance at the kitchen window. All the agents were in the backyard discovering bodies. No one was around to mind me.

Natural light surprised me as I opened the basement door. In the past, I had noticed the basement window from the outside. Tim questioned the purpose of its existence when we first moved. When he tried peering into it, cobwebs and dust blocked his view. We never thought to ask why our inside basement never had a window or the oddly modern brick wall that covered it.

The hazy sunlight wasn't enough to fully see my way down the steps. I flipped the switch from the top of the stairs. A big spark flew out of the light switch. The lights went out. I grabbed my phone from my pocket and pushed the flashlight application. The light it gave was only a fraction of light an actual flashlight could produce. Still it was a fair amount as I began my decent down the stair.

"Catherine, you don't want to go down there."

I looked behind me. Nothing. I moved my phone in front of me. There was nobody, not even an odd shadow. I continued to go down the stairs.

"Catherine!"

Chills went down my spine as I heard the familiar yet nonexistence voice. The voice of the one brother I've never got to hear. I shook my head. This was crazy. Jake's voice couldn't enter my head.

"Catherine Judith! If you know what is right for you, then you will listen to me! Don't go down there!"

With leaded legs, I continued to walk downstairs. Broken cement blocks gave way small area with a hanging light bulb and a dirty mattress. The perimeter had to only be three feet wide, a claustrophobic place for the children to be held.

I walked around the mattress soiled in misery and sin. There was plenty of destruction dust near the washer and dryer, but very little around the mattress. I realized then that the wall might have been put up to cover any evidence of Han's murders. There wasn't any more to see. The FBI already had the photographic evidence load in their vehicles.

I turned towards the stairs. A sort of small scratching sound emitted from my left heel. I turned and found the black backing with whiteboard relic of a Polaroid picture. I picked it out and flipped it to over.

There was the confirmation I never wanted. The Polaroid depicted my naked brother squatting on all four of his limbs. A Santa cap stood on his head. In between his distressed grimace held a candy cane like a rotten dog bone. Despite the few decades' worth of fading, I could still see tears down Jake's eye.

The air escaped my lungs. Everything went black.

15

I am sitting on the couch with the three children I dreamt of previously. The dark hair girl looks at me in horror. She nudges the black hair boy next to me. His eyes go wide. I turn to see the light-haired girl's mouth agape. "You're fading away…"

Suddenly, I am standing in the aisle of the sanctuary at First Evangelical of Stillwater. It's changed, expanded. At first, I'm embarrassed that I appear in the middle of the service before I quickly realize that everyone is oblivious to my presence as they sing hymns. I recognized a tall man in the middle of the pews. It's Uncle Oswald! He is sitting with Aunt Rebecca and Grandma Alice! She is wearing the pink velour track suit. Next to her is ME! Me, in my plaid Christmas jumper-I, realize I'm at Grandma Alice's last Christmas.
"Uncle Oswald?" My voice wasn't my own. It was deep yet childish. It was a boy's voice. "Grandma Alice? You are at church in a sweat suit?"
My eyes are fixated on my thirteen-year-old self. "Uncle Oswald and Aunt Rebecca had a daughter? I thought Aunt Rebecca couldn't have kids."
I am not Catherine now. I'm Jake!

We are back in Uncle Oswald car. I am sitting in between Grandma Alice and the girl. I look in the rearview mirror and run my hand through my short hair, a pointless action because I don't have a reflection. I hear the girl saying "We should visit my parents!"
The car drives up the familiar hill of Myrtle Ave before turning

onto Fifth Street North. As we pull up to my childhood house, I realize that the girl in the plaid jumper has the same parents I do.

I am surprised as I enter the dark house. It had the same furniture as the day I left it, but none of the lively festivities I remembered. Instead, my thirteen-year-old sister is yelling at some low life girl in the kitchen before she runs upstairs. Aunt Rebecca and Grandma Alice console the low life. I follow my sister. I want to see what else has changed.

I find my sister upstairs and can't believe who I see: my little brother Andrew nearly doubled my age.

Andrew wipes his brow on his flannel shirt. "Just clearing out this room for Mom now that she is back home."

I watch Catherine replying, "Is she better now?"

I watch Andrew's face contort as he packs boxes "Not exactly, she is in Dad's bedroom for the time being. You could say hi to her if you want."

I peer into the box Andrew is packing. It's full of pornographic magazines and my old copy of a Christmas Carol. Joe and Nick must have taken my copy for school because I wasn't here to read it. Those dogs!

My sister bounces out of the room. I see Andrew pulling out my book. "This does not look like it belongs here," Andrew mutters.

"You're right, it is actual literature," I say yet to realize my voice quickly disappears before it reaches my brother's ear.

I find my sister in our parent's room. To my dismay, I find a dishevel woman inhabiting my mother. My mom was never a fashion plate, but even in her mom jeans and plain T-shirts, she always looked together. She certainly never wore nightgowns or robes that have been packed in the attic since I could remember.

I watch my sister kiss Mom on the head and whisper, "He's coming home. You won't have to wait anymore."

Once again, my sister bounces out another room. I walk over to the old chaise lounge where Mom used to cuddle me and tell me stories. "Hi Mom," I say, "I'm home."

"Jake?" she whispers, "Where are you?"
"I'm here, besides you."

She looks at my direction, but I know she is only looking through me. "It's too cold outside. Do you have enough food? You should be home..."

"I'm home," I sigh, "The rest are not important anymore."

I suddenly appear outside where my dad is shouting at Uncle Oswald. "...You know where Joe is, Oswald? He's in jail again. I got the collect call yesterday morning! Nick, well, I don't know where Nick is. He jumped on a naval ship the minute he got the diploma. Jake is dead..."

I watch Catherine shout back "But he's not!"
Dad stubs his cigarette with an evil laugh. "Of course, he is! You were born a girl! Now get that worthless thing out of my sight!"
Uncle Oswald storms away grabbing my sister. I walk up to Dad. His hair thinned since the last morning I saw him leave for work. His flabby skin sinks into the crevices of his hollow face. Once Oswald is out of range, I watch Dad pull a half-drunk bottle of gin from the trash can. To my dismay, he chugs it as an athlete craving rehydration.
"This is what you became!" I shout, "A miserable drunk! Do not blame this on me! Don't blame it on her! Blame yourself!"
I pop back into the car as Uncle Oswald sits on the driver seat, slams the car door and mutters, "Whatever happened to Christmas being a time for miracles?"
I shake my head. "You don't know the half of it."

I walk around Grandma Alice's old lake house. Mostly, I had fond memories of the brothers and I goofing around here during the summer. The adults are in the sitting room that looks out at the lake. They talk about how cruel my father has become while drinking. Grandma Alice is trying to use my disappearance as an excuse. Uncle Oswald doesn't want to hear it. Frankly, I don't either.
I find my sister lying on the bed clutching a copy of "A Christmas Carol." The guest room looks nothing like I remember it. With the pink walls and white wicker furniture, it is evident that this is now a girl's room instead of a guest room.
"That's a good book," I say. "It helps if you open it."
Catherine silently mouths, "Stupid lousy prayer. Didn't work."
"It was you?" I ask her.
My sister stares up at the ceiling, oblivious to my questions.
"Yo, Sister, I came back. You prayed for my return; I am here."

I hear Grandma Alice's faint call, "Catherine. Can you come here?"

"Catherine? After Mom's middle name," I question as she walks out of the bedroom, "That is pretty."

I am back at Grandma Alice's house the cold February day we buried her. Uncle Oswald and Aunt Rebecca invited family members to eat the food the neighbors brought. I watch Catherine stand in the middle of the open kitchen accepting condolence wearing a hideous ruffle blouse underneath a vested black jumper. I look down at myself, thankful at least to have the clothes I wore when I was kidnapped.

Allen and Andrew walk in with Kirsten. Allen has a glassy eye look. Catherine smiles slyly.

"Allen, we didn't think you'd come."

"Now, is not the time to start, Catherine," Andrew warns.

"It's not polite to step into someone's home and criticize them, Andrew," Catherine said, "of course I don't fault you for your lack of decorum. You were raised by that drunken louse."

I see tears for in Allen's eyes. Catherine takes glee in her revenge from Christmas. "Pardon me for being so harsh, but the truth often is. This is my home because Grandma Alice made it so. You failed to provide me with such. When I leave for England, I'll leave the likes of you behind. Now, if you ever intended to do right by me as a father, kindly leave now."

"Catherine!" Andrew yells.

Allen already turns away. Kirsten follows him. Andrew walks to Uncle Oswald, probably to plea father's case. Even now, I don't hear their conversation. Uncle Oswald brushes Andrew away.

I look over at my smug sister. "Damn, Catherine," I say, "all those times watching 'Masterpiece Classics' with Grandma paid off."

I am now watching my fourteen-year-old sister pack for England while wearing jeans and a tie-dye shirt she made in art class the prior school year.

"Kids are wearing tie dye these days?" I ask.

Catherine remains oblivious to my presence.

"You know, when I was your age even though I am your age, actually, I am a year younger than you now." I snort, "Imagine that, my baby sister is now older than me. Anyways, you didn't want to be caught wearing tie-dye because that meant you were a dirty hippie in those days."

I watch Catherine pull out clothes from Dayton-Hudson's shopping bags into her new luggage.

"This place use to be a home, believe it or not. Probably more home to you than it was to me because you lived here. It's going to be sad when Uncle Oswald sells the house."

Catherine shuts the suitcase.

"So," I continue, "I initially thought I was called to meet Grandma Alice to the Great Beyond, but I have yet to see her. Maybe she is crossed over to join Grandpa Walter. I have never seen him. I haven't seen Grandma and Grandpa Shipley either. Anyways, since I am everywhere you are, I figure that I'm tied to you."

Aunt Rebecca knocks on the bedroom door. "Catherine, dinner."

"It's awesome we are going to England," I say. "I always wanted to leave Minnesota once in my life."

I see Catherine getting off the bus to boarding school. In front of the dormitory is Marguerite alive! She wears a pale green dress suit, and her blond hair is in the chignon. She greets Catherine with open arms.

As I witness the happy encounter, I uttered, "I guess she doesn't need me anymore."

I expect to fade away.

I sit in Marguerite's English class witnessing Catherine reading Anne Frank's Diary. A bratty boy pokes at her with his pen.

"Psst, why are you talking like you are from Sweden?"

I watch Catherine turn around. "I'm not."

"Theeeeeen, whaaaaaaaat's wiiiiiiiiiith theeeee looooooooong voooooooooweeeeeeels," the boy mocks. "Your name is Rhinelander. We know you are one of us."

A fat boy taps the dark-haired brat. "Hey, Tim, I don't think she is from The Isles. I think she is an American."

A cocky grin formed on the brat's face, "Which country?"

"America, you idiot," Catherine retorts.

"America, Rhinelander, is not a country. America is two continents. You must be from the so-called United States."

I watch Marguerite tower over Tim. "Is there a problem, Timlin?"

"This person from the United States called me an idiot!"

"If you don't wish for Miss Rhinelander to call you an idiot, may I suggest you behave a little less like your father?"

Tim snaps his fingers, "I was wondering why he was divorcing you..."

I say, "Now I know why I am still here, Catherine. I have to prevent you from ending up with that dirt bag."

I watch my sixteen-year-old sister stagger out of a pub into the streets with Tim's arm wrapped around her. Tim begins to kiss her neck.

"Don't do that!" Catherine screams.

"Why not," Sixteen-year-old Tim slurs, "You are so tasty."

Catherine pulls out a fake ID that bears the name and birth date of Emily Mulroney, "I'm your sister!"

Tim pulls out a card that bears my name and birth date but his ugly mug. "I thought you Americans marry your sister."

"Jake, another car is coming!"

Suddenly I am jumping into the street with a girl in a hospital gown. A very sober driver swerves away so he won't kill the children in front of him. He hits a lamp post.

Catherine and Tim watch as the man rambles about kids being in front of his car.

"There was nobody in front of your car, you drunk!" Tim shouts.

"Stupid drunk drivers," Catherine slurs, "they are so irresponsible!"

I turn to the girl in the hospital gown. "Thanks, Emily."

"I think the next time I'll let the idiots get hit by the car so they can finally learn something about responsibility."

I am back in my dormitory at Middlesex University watching my twenty-two-year-old sister studying for mid-terms. The phone rings.

"Hello," Catherine answers, "Tim? Tim? Timlin! What is wrong? Marguerite? No, she is not dead....I talked to her yesterday. We are to have lunch tomorrow...A drunken bogger? Tim, this is no time to be derogatory....What? She was hit by a car!"

Catherine slams the phone down onto the receiver. I try to comfort her, but she can't feel my touch.

"Maybe you should go to Ireland," I say.

As if she heard me Catherine suddenly stuffs random clothes in her rucksack and heads out the door.

I am waiting outside of Timlin's old bedroom in his father's house. Marguerite appears in her Burberry coat she died in. Her arms are crossed.

"This is how my favorite pupil and my step-son honor me! Of all the...."

A golden light shines through the door. I grab Marguerite's hand.

"I've seen this before. A new soul has been created."

"My word," Marguerite gasps.

I am watching Catherine going through labor nine months later in Tim's Dublin flat. Tim is rubbing his arm because she grabbed him so tightly. His old girlfriend is the midwife. Marguerite is watching by me.

"She ought to be at a hospital," Marguerite mutters.

"She's supposed to be back in the United States," I mention, "Her VISA is up."

A baby starts wailing. There is the disgustedly beautiful baby boy still cover in the vertex.

"Ah, he is a beautiful Christmas baby," the midwife coos.

"Christmas?" the new mother questions.

"Yes, it's Christmas Eve," the midwife answers as she puts Jacob his mother's arms.

"Welcome to the world, Jacob Marley Rhinelander."

"Uh, Ketty," Tim said, "I was going to give him my name."

"Welcome to the world, Jacob Marley Mulroney."

"Catherine, that is not my name."

"Shut up, Timlin; I just gave birth...."

"She just been through labor," the midwife says, "leave her be. Besides, Jacob is a lovely name."

Time passes. Marguerite's spirit has gone off to be with family for the holidays. I see Tim and Catherine sleeping. Jacob is swaddled next to his mother on the mattress. I walked over to him.

"Hi, Little Buddy," I whisper, "I'm your Uncle Jake. I think Jacob is a perfect name for you too. You know, 'A Christmas Carol' is one of my favorite books. Jacob Marley is a good name for you."

Baby Jacob opens his eyes.

"I always wanted a sister. That is why I hang around your mom. I always liked kids too. I'll never get to have my own, but seeing you grow up...I can't wait. I know you can't see me, but I am always going to be with you always."

Baby Jacob's little arm escapes his poorly constructed swaddle. He reaches over to me.

We return to Valley City. I enter the house first walking through the wall. Nadine is braiding her long dark hair. Robbie is conjuring an old cartoon that has long since been canceled. Lindsay sits at the kitchen table waiting for a piece of cake she knows she'll never receive. Jacob bursts through the front door and runs all over the living room. Pregnant Catherine is entering the front door. All of my fellow spirits' eyes fixate on me. Lindsay speaks, "You came back, why?"

I point to Catherine, "She's my sister. She lives here now."

Jacob is now shooting hockey pucks in the driveway. He is lifting the back end of the stick too high.

"That is not how you shoot," I say.

Jacob turns to me. "How do you shoot?"

"Keep the stick on the ground," I say, "you don't need to swing it high. It's hockey, not golf."

We play. It's natural. It's like I am alive again.

"He saw you!" Lindsay exclaims as I watch Jacob sleep.

"It was cool," I say.

"It was," Lindsay agrees, "he can help us."

"How?"

"You can tell him where we are buried."

"What good will that do?"

"It may free us."

I snort, "Will we ever truly be free?"

"Not if you don't tell him where we are."

I shake my head. "He thinks I'm a real kid."

"You were..."

"Look!" I shout, "For eternity I have watched my family without being able to connect with them! Now I can connect with my nephew! He is not going to want anything to do with me after he figures out that I am a ghost! I won't tell him!"

Lindsay slumps through the door to the hall. I can sense Regina's and Robbie's disapproval from the other side of the wall.

It has snowed in Valley City. Jacob is shooting the puck across the slippery street. A black sports car starts turning into the street. It's a different car that the one he had over thirty years ago, but I know it is him. Jacob sees him and steps into the yard.

"Get into the house!" I yell!

"Why?" Jacob asks.

"Just do it! Go in and don't answer the door!"

Jacob goes in. Unfortunately, he wasn't quick enough. My murderer sees him entering the house. Lindsay appears.

"He still comes. The old woman always turned him away, but he still came back. Now the old lady isn't here anymore."

"You're a ghost," I say, "Scare him off!"

"The only person who has ever seen any of us is your nephew. He can be the one to help us seek justice."

"Our killer won't come back once he realizes that his mother is no longer here to cover for him."

Lindsay looks towards the window of Jacob's room. "I think he has more of an incentive to return now."

I walk through the bedrooms. Jacob is sleeping. Maggie is sleeping. I see Tim and Catherine asleep in their bed with books in their laps. Suddenly I hear Regina cry, "He's here!"

I appear by the living room window with the other three children. Our killer is crossing the yard from the side. The motion sensing lights in the Schuler's yard go out as he passes their deck. He turns and starts to run.

"He was going to uproot me," Robbie says.

"Why do you say that?" I ask.

"Because I am buried in the shed and that was where he was going to," Robbie says.

"Make sense," Regina sighs. "You were the one he didn't bury in the open. His mother was starting to catch on to his lie about attempting to catch moles when you arrived. If you are unearthed, then it is one less body they discover."

I snort, "Like anyone is going to dig up bodies."

Regina looks at me, "Haven't you been listening?"

Lindsay shakes her head, "He never has."

It's Sunday Morning. A clamor of blend voices fulfills my head. It isn't my family nor the spirits I sit with. "What is going on?" I ask.

"Prayers," Lindsay says.

"Make it stop!"

"There is only one way how," Regina says.

Jacob is outside shooting the puck against the garage. The voices in my head have grown louder. They are all saying, "Please find Mrs. Mulroney's brother."

"Hey, Jacob!" I call.

Jacob runs over to me. "Are you going to take me to the river to practice shooting today, Jake?"

"Your mother would never let you go that far," I answer.

Jacob frowns.

"Speaking of your mother, what to help me get her Christmas

present?"

"She already has her present," Jacob remarks. "Dad bought her the chenille blanket she wanted."

"Are you sure she wants a blanket?"

"That's what she asks for."

"You're wrong," I say. "I know what she really wants. It's buried in the backyard."

Jacob leans close to me, "Like treasure?"

"If you want to call it that..."

I am watching Catherine lying in a hospital bed shaking my head. I warn her not to go downstairs, yet she went in anyways. All those horrible pictures...nothing good came from her seeing them.

****

I woke up. Jake stood at the foot of my hospital bed. Staring into his eyes as he faded away, I realized the dreams were real. The prayers worked. He had been with me the whole time! Although he was no longer visible, I knew he was still there, and always will be.

16

The doctors and nurses were not forthcoming how I ended up in the hospital, nor were willing to give me any indication when I was to be released. Judith visited me the evening I woke up. She carefully evaded any questions I had about Jake's case. The only things she spoke about were my children, assuring that they were safe with Tim back at the Inn.

The next morning the doctor overseeing my case told me that I was to see a psychologist to determine that my episode of shock didn't result in any mental maladies. I waited in a sterile white room with metal furniture. To my surprise, Dr. Roman Gubler walked in.

He wore a vintage tweed suit this time, although he still didn't look like a doctor. He walked in briskly, set his laptop down on the table across from me immediately typing before he sat down. There was no trace of the gentile doctor who met my son.

"I thought you were a child's psychologist," I said.

Without removing his eyes from the computer, Dr. Gubler replied, "In a small state as North Dakota, a practitioner either has to work in various disciplines of his field or endure long car trips across the country. In my case, I must do both to make it as a forensic psychologist."

"North Dakota has a forensic psychologist?" I asked. "I didn't realize that we had that many serial killers."

Dr. Gubler answered curtly, "I work in the entire Midwest."

Dr. Gubler continued to type on his laptop and flipped through a manila folder he pulled from his briefcase. I sat with my hands clasped on the table in his view.

"Is my family still under suspicion?" I asked.

"Nope," answered Dr. Gubler, "The evidence found in the bricked up corner of your basement alone would have locked Han up from life."

"Would have?"

Dr. Gubler gave me a sad look. "Catherine, Cody Han is dead."

"Recently?" I replied.

"Since yesterday," Dr. Gubler answered. "The FBI tracked him in Colorado. From what I have been told, he committed suicide by cop. He probably figured what his future inmates had in store for him if he went quietly. He ran outside bearing arms and shooting at the agents' direction, injuring one."

"I don't think his chances in hell are any better," I remarked.

Dr. Gubler looked at me astonished. "No, I don't think he would fare well in hell."

"Of course, he could refuse to cross over," I continued, "but then he would have four angry spirits of the children to contend with. If his path crosses with the spirit of my Grandma Alice, may the devil have mercy on his soul."

"Among others..."

"Did the FBI found remains of other children?""

"No; however, they found evidence at his Colorado residence similar to what the FBI has found in your basement. Some of it links to a missing boy in New Mexico. That is all I know and more than I should share."

"Have the FBI check missing children reports from all of the surrounding states," I mentioned, "He seemed to have an excellent mode of operation going for him of kidnapping across state lines."

"There is more you need to know," said Dr. Gubler, "Gladys Han is dead too."

Dr. Gubler stared at me. I stared at him waiting for information about Gladys Han's death. He sat in silence. I knew he was waiting for a reaction I didn't know how to give. Given that I was seated in a white hospital room wearing scrubs, I knew damn well that the confusion I felt was not the appropriate response if I wanted to be deemed suitable for discharge.

Dr. Gubler sighed. "No, the FBI didn't track her down and killed her if that is what you are thinking."

I shook my head. "No, it's not. I hardly knew the woman. Never knew anything about her. I paid my rent through a realtor; therefore, I never had any contact with her to form an opinion."

Dr. Gubler tapped his fingers on the table. "Fair enough, now let's get to the point. The cops found you blacked out while clutching evidence you were never meant to see. When the cops found you, you were presumed dead because you soiled yourself. You were unconscious for thirty-six hours. It is quite evident you experienced neurological trauma from shock. Yet, you look completely fine sitting in front of me."

"I feel completely fine."

"Catherine, I have worked in the field of psychology for a while now. Everyone I have seen claimed they are fine. Most tend to appear the part, yet, beneath the façade, there's mental illness."

"Having a dead brother doesn't mean I am mentally ill," I replied flatly.

"True, but your recent chain of behaviors doesn't indicate you were in your right mind. You willfully went to your place of residence when the police told you to stay away. You continued to enter your house after the county sheriff explained how gruesome photographs identified other bodies that were being dug up. You view the said photographs of your brother's final moments. I'll just put it bluntly, who in their right mind does that?"

I shrugged. "All I ever knew of Jake was that he was my dead brother. At the time, I figured if his death was all I would ever know of him, I might as well learn everything about it."

"At the time?"

I leaned forward and started Dr. Gubler in the eye. "If you are looking to lock me up for being crazy, Dr. Gubler, fine I'll give you the statement you want. I saw Jake."

Dr. Gubler pushed his laptop away. With his hands folded in front of him on the table, he repeated, "You saw Jake."

"Yes," I said, "When I woke up in the hospital he was there. It was to confirm that he really was in my brain showing me what had happened."

"I am going to need you to explain more, Catherine."

"When I was thirteen, our grandmother was dying of cancer. She raised me since before I could remember. The Christmas before she died, I had this insane notion in my head that if Jake suddenly reappeared she would heal. I thought Jake magically coming back for Christmas would cure all the family's ill. So, I prayed at church for Jake to come home."

Dr. Gubler's face soften, "You must have been devastated when he didn't."

"I was because I didn't know he returned."

"He did?"

"Yes, Jake appeared right at my Grandmother's church as I hoped he would. I couldn't see him because I can't see the dead like Jacob can."

"Interesting," Dr. Gubler replied.

"After I blacked out, I was back at that church on that Christmas. I just wasn't me. I was looking at me sitting with my grandma in the pew. I was Jake. He came back. My students were right, prayer works."

Dr. Gubler shifted in his chair, reminding me of Uncle Oswald tipping back in his chair when someone fibbed, and he knew it. Yet, Uncle Oswald always had a whimsical look on his face. Dr. Gubler's face remained stoic.

"You don't understand, Dr. Gubler, all these events that have occurred this week have been a freaking miracle!"

"A miracle?"

"Look, in order stay out of mental institutions and off drugs, I had to force myself to accept that that we would never know what happened to Jake and just block him out of my mind..."

"That would be easy enough for you," Dr. Gubler cut in, "He disappeared before you were born."

"Not really. I had this anger towards my family for knowing Jake whereas I got robbed of the opportunity. It's complicated. I thought I stuffed it well until a student told me miracles happen through Jesus, and well, all that fury got unleashed in a lecture my about how miracles weren't real. Little did I know they were! My students prove it!"

"Through a mass prayer, I heard all about it. It is all the town has talked about."

"There was never any evidence that he was buried in North Dakota. I moved to this town into Hans' house not knowing I was among spirits for the past two years. My students prayed and all the gruesome answers about Jake's kidnapping appeared. How is that not a miracle?!"

Dr. Gubler stared at me, suppressing whatever emotion his profession wouldn't let him express. A still and deafening silence filled the room. Then the tears started rolling down my face.

"I know you think I am crazy for saying the discovery of Jacob's body is a miracle," I cried, "Ideally, my prayer would have resulted in Jake coming home alive saying some farm family cared for him while he recovered from amnesia. My life never was a sappy Christmas television special. I know children who are kidnapped are often murdered. After thirty some years of having nothing, my family has answers, they have a body to bury, and I know he came back to me in spirit the Christmas I prayed for him. All of this is more than I ever wished to hope for ever!"

Dr. Gubler took a tissue out of his pocket. "It must have been nice knowing that he came back that Christmas when you prayed after believing otherwise."

"He stayed," I continued. "He followed me to England. He returned to Valley City just because my family moved here. During that time, he came across Tim's sister, Emily and stepmother, Marguerite. They all were there. People don't leave when they died."

"I know," Dr. Gubler said.

"You know?" I said, "Tim and I thought when the FBI told us Jacob had to meet with you that you were going to commit him to the mental institution. Ironically, you have been the biggest advocate that his visions of Jake were real."

"They were," he said.

"But aren't psychologists supposed to tell patients ghost don't exist," I argued.

"That is only an assumption," Dr. Gubler. "I was just to evaluate whether Jacob had disillusion disorders or not. He tested out as not."
"But you argued with my husband that ghost were very real. Why?"

Dr. Gubler shifted in his chair. "When my mom was pregnant with me,I had a brother named Maxwell, named after my mother's father. Three months before I was born, Grandpa Max and my brother were to drive to their annual fishing trip to Lake Tahoe. They never made it out of Las Vegas. A drunk driver hit them, killing them both."

"Oh my god! I am so sorry! How old was your brother?"

"Nine. I was born the day after what would have been his tenth birthday. My mom told me that the day he died, all he was talking about was that it would be so cool to take me fishing. He hoped that we shared the same birthday so we could have a big celebration. He really wanted to be the cool teenage older brother. I know what it is like being cheated out of a brother; however, I don't understand what you are going to a point."

"You are telling me that you never had the urge to look at car crashes."

"Noooo," Dr. Gubler shook his head. "If fact, when I went to college, my brother would show up warning me about the drunk drivers out there. I never saw a crash, but like Jacob, I saw a ghost. I have disclosed more about myself than I should."

We sat there in silence but alas it was comfortable. Then there was a knock at the door.

"So, Catherine, do you feel as if you are crazy and unstable?"

"I have never felt so at peace in my life," I said. "All I needed was proof that prayer worked."

"That's good enough for me," said Dr. Gubler as he walked to the door. "Well, just one more thing. I have been curious, why did you name your son after Jacob Marley from 'A Christmas Carol'?"

I chuckled, "If my students wouldn't have interrupted me they would have heard a lecture about of Jacob Marley resembled redemption and everlasting friendship in his appearance to Scrooge."

Dr. Gubler cocked his head, "Is that all, Catherine?"

"Of course."

"I found it ironic that Jacob Marley had the same first name as your dead brother."

I sighed in both amazement and frustration that Dr. Gubler could get to the bottom of my soul. "That Christmas I prayed, my brother, Andrew, found Jake's old copy of 'A Christmas Carol' and gave it to me. I like how Jacob Marley came back to Scrooge when he really had no reason to other than their friendship. Somehow, it gave me hope that my Jake would return although I'd never admit that to myself."

"That's beautiful," Dr. Gubler said. He opened the door. "She's not crazy, let's get her discharged."

Judy drove me back to the Wagon Wheel Inn still in hospital scrubs. Many of the staff nodded in our direction as we entered the building and walked towards our room. I clutched my bag of soil clothes as if it were a security blanket until I reached the safety of my room. The kids were quietly playing with their Christmas presents. Tim was sitting at the table reading scripts. Judy steadied me on the bed. "Let her rest," she quipped to Tim.

The moment the door clicked behind Judy, Tim muttered, "God, Catherine, not once in my life did I ever feel the urge to visit a cancer ward and watch kids die just because my sister had cancer."

A smiled formed in my mouth. Tim would never treat me as the invalid everyone thought I was. I loved him for that.

"Well, I saw Emily and you haven't," I taunted

"Excuse me," Tim said.

"Remember the time we were coming out of the pub using fake cards?"

"Which time?"

I leaned back on the pillow and laughed. "I don't know, but I do know all those drunken drivers we kept seeing were spooked not drunk."

Tim shrugged and went back to his script.

It was a cold Sunday afternoon. Everyone stood in front of city hall in their Sunday best. On the street were four small coffins strapped on trucks. The mayor stood at the top of the step.

"Cody Han was born a citizen of the United States. As a citizen of the United State of North Dakota, he had the right to live without unlawful seizure even though the majority of the citizens suspected his sinister nature. We ask the family of the victims of Cody Han to accept our condolence and our sincere regret that the crimes against their loved ones occurred in our town without our knowledge. The town wishes to gift each family with a coffin and paid for the burial cost. I also want to address to the city of Valley City that we do not handle threats to our citizens' safety lightly. I ask the townspeople to be diligent and proactive. If you know of abuse, do not sweep it under the rug. These crimes are never to occur in this town again! Now it is time to send Jacob Rhinelander, Lindsay Briar, Nadine Tucker, and Robbie Hunt to their rightful homes with the promise that no children in Valley City will meet their fate!"

The trucks rev up and drove off to their compass directions. Judy was in the truck heading East finally taking her son home to Stillwater. My family followed the herd going to the Valley Lutheran Church where Gladys Han's memorial service was to be held. Somehow, I ended up following Stiejim and a red headed lady.

"I told you he was no good," the woman said.

"Not now, Linda" Stiejim gruffed.

"You think I drove eighty miles to see small coffins. No, I came here to tell you, 'I told you so' and to pay my respects to Gladys."

"Why didn't you bring Gloria?"

"She was driving with a group over to the Cities to catch a Lynx game. She ought to be having fun with her peers instead of seeing this horrible sight."

Stiejim grunted.

"You know there is a position with the Moorhead Police Department available if you want to see her more often."

"There are many good neighborhoods in Valley City."

Tim snickered, catching the attention of Stiejim and his ex-wife. Stiejim slowed his step. Tim greeted Linda, charming her with his Irish borough. Tim and Linda walked ahead with the children. Stiejim stared at me.

"You are coming to the service?"

"If that is alright with you...."

"It's a public service for anyone who wishes to pay their respects."

"And she was your sister," I commented, "After you have allowed us to live in her home and all you have done in Jake's case, it was the least I could do. This town rallies around its people."

"That they do," Stiejim said as we walked up the church steps.

17

Stillwater has always been a beautiful city. There is a quaint Main Street with antique and specialty stores and gourmet restaurants next to the river front. I just never got to appreciate its beauty. Stilwater was forever tainted by the memories of Jake's disappearance. Now I visit virtually every night. Tonight I sit on the community deck overlooking the Saint Croix River. Leaning against the white railing is Jake, in his mid-forties as he should be. We watch the snow fall on the skeletal tree branches on the Wisconsin side of the river, neither of us feeling the cold.

"Thanks for coming," he says.

"I never miss our nightly meetings," I say.

Jake chuckles, "I meant to thank you for coming to my memorial services. I know Mom dragged you there kicking and screaming."

"Now I wouldn't say that..."

It was true. The only reason I drove the family to Stillwater was that

Mom promised to buy Tim and I tickets to a play at the Guthrie Theatre. My plan was to sit in the back of the church and make a quick escape at the end. The plan failed the moment my children met their cousins and young aunt. They demanded to sit with them in the front pews during the service. Of course, Andrew and Nick wanted to know the strange woman walking in with our mother. The moment Allen overheard my mom introducing me to Andrew and Nick as their sister....

"You should have seen your face when Dad wrapped you up in the biggest hug," Jake laughs, "your eyes nearly bulged out of your socket!"

"Like a little squeeze toy," I comment. "You said that yesterday and the day before I might add."

Jake shrugs. "Are you coming back to Stillwater?"

"I already got the invitation to the Rhinelander family reunion in June."

"Stillwater is incredible in the summer. Wished I didn't die as a kid so I could go pub crawling..."

"We could do it tomorrow night," I suggested.

"It's not the same," Jake says.

We stare out onto the river as it carried chunks of ice off to the South. The sun glitters on the ice creating a scene magical enough to smooth over feelings of woe.

"Are you coming into Valley City today?"

"Got to," Jake answers, "I need to teach Jake how to score from halfway across the rink during his recess. He's doing well so far. You really need to sign him up for hockey next year."

"Maybe by then I'll change Tim's mind about the sport."

Jake leans back from the railing then turns to go.

"You better wake up soon. You have to finish that lesson on 'A Christmas Carol.'"

"Yes, I do. Are you going to be here tomorrow?"

"Wouldn't miss it? It's nice finally to have a relationship one of my sisters. You're the only woman in my afterlife."

"What about my sister-in-law, Emily?"

Jake shrugs. "She's nice, but a little high maintenance. I guess it runs in her family, don't cha know?"

"I know," I agreed.

"Eventually, I'll cross over and see Grandma Alice again," Jake mentioned, "but now I am just not ready. I am having too much fun with my nephew."

I'll never be ready for you to cross over. "We all enjoy knowing that you are still around," I say, "please stay as long as you like."

Jake walks through the railing and onto the river. I watch until he fades away.

I woke up in a daze. At first confused where I was until I realized I was at my new house.

*****

Gladys Han named Stiejim, her sole heir. His first order of business was to tear down her house. Within hours of his sister's memorial, he came over to deliver the eviction notice.

"You certainly don't want to live where live your brother was murdered, now, do you?"

Not in the house where Jake was killed, but I wouldn't dare dream of moving out of Valley City. There were too many people I cared living here. Unfortunately, there weren't too many places Tim and I could afford.

"Where else are we going to live?" I asked as I stared as the notice.

"I know of a place that will be vacant in twenty-four hours," Stiejim replied.

Stiejim packed minimal belongings that night and headed an hour east to Moorhead, Minnesota. As he explained as Tim and I signed the rental agreement to his house, "I love Valley City, but I am a father first. Now that Gladys is gone and doesn't need me to watch after her, I need to go Moorhead and make things right with Gloria."

Stiejim agreed to give my family the house on a rent-to-own basis. Until we owned it, we had to keep Stiejim's furniture and hunting trophies in the house. I wasn't wowed about having my morning coffee with a taxidermy deer head staring at me from the kitchen wall; still, it was better than living in Cody Han's house of horrors.

The house was closer to the Junior/Senior High School and the majority of my students. Tim dropped off the kids at their schools on his way to the university so that I could walk to school. Tim, never possessing the patience I had with the children, didn't like the change in routine.

"Catherine! Where is Maggie coat?" he cried from upstairs in Maggie's room.

"In the hall closet where it is supposed to be!" I shouted from the entryway. "Now hurry up! I got Jacob already for you and I'm running late!"

Tim swore in Gaelic. Jacob gasped.

"Mum, did you hear what Dad said?"

"Don't listen to your father," I said. "Just listen to your Uncle Jake when he comes to teach you how to shoot the puck today." Lowering my voice to a whisper, "We are signing you up for hockey next year. Just be hushed about it."

Jacob put his finger to his lip.

"Tim, Maggie, I am leaving!" I shouted. "I love you."

Bending down to kiss Jacob, I said, "I love you too. Be good."

I opened the door to find the usual sight of a student on my doorstep…

"Hi, Mrs. Mulroney, Spankey here, selling pretzels for the Episcopalians."

"Pretzels, now? What kind?"

"The hard kind," Spankey answered. "You know, the ones covered in salt. We also have the chocolate covered kind and some that have this honey mustard dust covering them."

"Put me down for a box of the chocolate covered pretzels, Spankey."

"Really? Only one? I mean, Spankey's church did pray for you and all."

I sighed. That guilt trip persuaded me from buying three magazines subscriptions from Leif Wilson, two canisters of popcorn from Amy Tinklebaum, and five boxes of cookie dough from Mia Vellon. All were supporting their churches.

"Okay, Spankey, make that two boxes of the chocolate covered pretzels and a box of the honey mustard kind."

Spankey scribbled on her order form. "Thank you, Mrs. Mulroney!"

I smiled, hoping one of these days a student's church sell chocolate bars as a fundraiser.

Returning to the school after winter break was like walking back in time before Christmas. Students were talking in the halls and scurrying over to class the moment the bell rang. I was content with the normalcy. For my first six classes, I had the students watch a brief movie that sagwayed into this month's lesson. My last class of the day had another lecture.

Kids sat down without placing their notebooks out on the desk. Facing the chalkboard, I snickered at their assumption.

"Good Afternoon, Class," I greeted as I wrote on the board, "We will be picking up where we left off prior to Winter Break."

A clamor of groans and "Ah, really?" filled the air.

"I thought we were watching a movie," Trent whined.

"Your other classes did," Mia pointed out.

"We're talking about 'A Christmas Carol'?" asked Amy, "it's not even Christmas anymore!"

On the chalkboard I scripted, "Who Prayed for Scrooge?" With that, my students turned from complaining teenagers to thoughtful thinkers. With serious faces, everyone pulled their pens and notebooks out of their backpacks.

"Last class, I thought I was giving a lesson in great literature. However, it was I who ended up learning a lesson from all of your prayers. I didn't know it at the time, but the prayer I said when I was thirteen worked. Jake came back in spirit; but, since he didn't miraculously come back alive like they do in movies, I didn't accept that the prayer worked. As gruesome as it was, finding Jake's body was a miracle. Everyone in my family long gave up ever knowing the truth of what happened to him. If all of you had not prayed, I still wouldn't know the answer and never have the chance to make peace with my brother's death. I thank you and my family thanks you."

The class met me with murmurs of "You're welcome."

"It got me thinking that Ebenezer Scrooge being visited by the three Ghosts of Christmas was a miracle. They presented him insight of his life which abled him to change his greedy ways. Yet, would the spirits have visited any mere mortal by chance?"

The students either shrugged or shook their heads.

"Of course not! Someone had to have prayed for Scrooge for the Ghosts of Christmases to give him a chance. Now who do you think prayed for him?"

"It was Jacob Marley," Mia answered. "How else did he know that the ghosts were coming?"

"Good point, Mia. Now can anyone tell me why Jacob Marley prayed for Scrooge?"

"Because he was his best friend," Leif answered.

"Because he was gay for Scrooge," Trent called out.

"There may be truth to your point, Trent," I commented, "however; I do believe you said that with the intent of being vulgar. That I am not going to tolerate."

"How about his nephew, Fred?" Amy suggested, "He loved Scrooge enough to invited toast to him at every Christmas party even though he always turned down the invitation."

"Another good point made by Amy!" I declared, "Any others? Holly, do you have any input to who could have prayed for Scrooge?"

Holly gave me her all too familiar smirked. "Mrs. Mulronney, I mean no disrespect, however, I feel that it is pointless to debate who prayed for Scrooge when he is long dead and Christmas is over. There are many people who need our prayers right now. Since you now know the power of prayer, I was wondering if you would allow me to lead the class into one."

"Oh yeah, Mr. Branson was in a car accident on I-94," Amy mentioned, "Someone was texting while driving and swerved into his lane."

"It's really bad," Mia confirmed. "His leg got mangled. I heard that it is going to take multiple operations to fix it."

"So can we pray for Mr. Branson, Mrs. Mulroney?"

Federal law didn't allow that for it violated the separation of church and state. North Dakota being a conservative state was quite liberal in following that rule.

"Holly, I don't think anyone will object if you pray. Am I right class?"

The class bowed their heads and folded their hands. Momentarily, fog formed into Jake. With a wink from him, I understood I was watching another miracle setting in motion.

Dear Readers,

It would be a lie to say that the Jacob Wetterling case didn't partially inspire this story. He was abducted a year after my family moved to Minnesota. The case has stuck with me along with the entire state for decades. I couldn't think of another name for Catherine's missing brother other than Jacob or Jake. I also thought about Adam Welsh, the boy whose kidnapping changed how America dealt with missing children cases. Adam's siblings never got to know him alive as Catherine never got to know Jake.

I worked in Valley City, ND the year after I graduated from Minnesota State University Moorhead. It is one of the few towns I could think of where the entire town would unite in prayer. I enjoyed making mental visits to the city as I wrote this book. I also have a deep love for Stillwater, MN. I hope neither town gets mad at me for using their location as a backdrop to a gruesome crime. Writing allows me to visit the places I love.

I don't know what possessed me to sit down one Christmas night and begin to write this story. I consider how the book suddenly popped into my head to be a gift from above. I wrote it out with hope for those whose families have experienced tragedy as the Rhinelanders will eventually find comfort as Catherine did.

Sincerely,

S.Collin Ellsworth